THE EQUALIZER

A novel by David Deutsch

Based on the Universal television series
THE EQUALIZER
Created by Michael Sloan

Adapted from the episodes 'The Equalizer' by Michael
Sloan and 'The Children's Song' by W. K. Scott Meyer,
Joel Surnow, and Maurice Hurley

A STAR BOOK
Published by
the Paperback Division of
W.H. Allen & Co Plc

A Star Book
Published in 1986
by the Paperback Division of
W.H. Allen & Co Plc
44 Hill Street, London W1X 8LB

Printed and bound in Great Britain by
Anchor Brendon Ltd, Tiptree, Essex

ISBN 0–352 31948–8

equal·iz·er /*n*/: one that equalizes: as **a**: a device that provides for equal distribution (as of force) **b**: a score that ties a game

ONE

To any seasoned, weary New Yorker in the vicinity of Park Avenue and 42nd Street that evening, there appeared to be nothing unusual about the rush-hour chaos. Traffic jammed the crosswalks, causing gridlock despite the furious efforts and flailing hand signals of a NYPD cop trying to untangle the mess. Frenzied pedestrians, all seemingly late for something, squeezed between the bumpers to navigate from one side of the street to the other. Cab drivers yelled, and everyone with a horn leaned on it. The cacophony flew in the face of traffic signs warning drivers of fines for honking and 'blocking the box'. Signs meant nothing in the streets of Manhattan; here, it was survival of the fittest.

The imposing modern glass and steel box-like tower of the Pan Am Building, its checkerboard of lights blazing, was a mere backdrop to the early evening chaos. It was Grand Central Station – the massive brown stone, vaulted nineteenth-century monument which had survived all attempts at demolition – that persisted as the heart through which the life of the area flowed. Refugees from office high

7

rises throughout Manhattan pushed through the doors of the weathered railway terminal while beleaguered, arriving out-of-town passengers, dazed from the swirling confusion, battled their way against the flow towards the exits. Businessmen in shades of grey, black, and charcoal, moved like mechanical mannequins who deftly dodged oncoming passengers. Possessed of natural homing instincts, they streamed towards the commuter gates to catch the 6.20 to Darien or the 6.37 to Stamford. So set was the routine for most of them, that individual faces had ceased to exist, instead melting into a single impressionistic blur which blended into the human landscape of the station.

Even the more recent changes in the vast chamber of the grand old terminal went largely unnoticed by most of the rush-hour regulars. True, the small bank branch was still there on the terminal's main floor, but now the automatic teller machine handled most of its transactions. Beyond the bank in the Lexington Arcade, the pretzel vendor had given way to another gourmet chocolate chip cookie concession. On the station's lower level, the famous Oyster bar was still doing a booming business, although escalating prices had since made oysters off limits for the average commuter.

Those with time to kill clustered around the bar near the bank of doors at the station's Vanderbilt Avenue entrance, where they yelled in hopes of catching the bartender's eye, sneaked glances at a late-breaking story in a bystander's paper, or prophesied to friends and outright strangers the outcome of tonight's Knicks game. Meanwhile, the booming speakers announced changes in schedules, track numbers, and train arrivals. Mixed with the thunder of footsteps, the babble of voices, and the noise of street traffic, these announcements were little more than a blaring jumble of notes which drifted upwards and vanished into the vaulted blue ceiling where they were lost in its painting of the night sky with its illuminated constellations; even so, passengers needing information mobbed the small information booth in the centre of the station. Above the human stampede, the giant, glaringly bright Kodak billboard advertised cameras and film to capture the moment: 'Because time goes by'.

Three men dressed in Ivy League vested suits glanced nervously at their watches and appeared very aware of the time going by. One was travelling quickly through the main terminal in the area where gates led to the train platforms below. The second agent prowled the great station lobby from a perch by the upper level bar from which he could view the activity on the main floor. The third in the trio waited anxiously at the entrance to another platform.

The first of these shadowy men, Mason – the one in the grey three-piece suit who lurked outside the gate barriers – stood rigid with tension as one of the commuter trains arrived and disgorged its passengers into the terminal. Tall, serious, his hair greying at the temples, Mason looked like any other business executive in pin stripes – except for the curious fact that he was speaking softly into what resembled a matchbook. The small device, actually a radio, picked up his words without transmitting the noise of voices and other extraneous sounds. Leaning on the balustrade overlooking the terminal floor, Mason's colleague and fellow agent, Tom Hellman, spoke similarly into the palm of his hand. Both men scanned the crowd emerging from the platform stairwell. At the barrier of a nearby staircase, the third agent, a shorter, muscular man with piercing eyes, received the transmissions and acknowledged them with a subtle sign to the other members of his team. No one bothered to take any notice of the agents talking to their hands. This was, after all, New York City.

On the station platform below the gate entries, a man in his late twenties stepped out of the train and surveyed the crowd warily. His olive, pock-marked skin and dark Cuban features were clouded with tension. His thin lips pressed together, forming a taut line, while his dark brown eyes darted about. Though he wore a jacket and tie and carried a thin leather briefcase, his movements were out of keeping with the respectable image his wardrobe sought to convey.

9

He moved like an ocean scavenger hiding behind rock after rock, his path erratically moving between openings in the crowd. He hurried up the stairs, took a sharp right, and headed west towards another train platform; in doing so, he eluded Mason's glance. Tom Hellman missed him too. Only Anson was left to intercept him at the barrier.

As the Cuban was about to pass Anson at the stairwell entrance, his eye zeroed in on a glint of light coming from underneath Anson's open coat. An agent – he was sure of it. He could make out the butt of the agent's gun in his shoulder holster as it caught the light. The young, furtive Cuban – whose name was Carolides – was acutely tuned to catch such details. His eye leaped from the gun to another reflection, this one the tiny radio transmitter in the palm of Anson's hand. Anson's eyes locked with Carolides'. Panic gripped the Cuban. Seized by the fear common to cornered quarry, he let loose with a cry which welled up from his throat. Anson stepped towards him. Carolides suddenly pushed the woman in front of him towards the agent and bolted past him, shoving others in front of him out of his way.

Then he saw his ticket out of here.

She was a girl – a blonde teenager in a parochial high school uniform who stumbled in front of him. Without missing a beat, Carolides reached down and yanked her up; with his other hand, he grabbed a knife from inside his coat. A woman in the crowd saw the shining blade pressed against the girl's throat and let out a scream, which mingled with the girl's own helpless cry. The girl, who held her breath as if it might be her last, screamed and kicked, then ceased to struggle when she felt the cold steel against her throat. Carolides pushed her down the stairs to the platform.

Propelling the girl forward, Carolides bulldozed his way through the passengers who scurried to catch the overdue train. Meanwhile, Mason jumped at the sudden commotion at the top of the west stairwell. An alarm sounded inside his head. After spotting the terrorist and his hostage, he relayed a message into his matchbook radio: 'Heading down the west staircase, a young girl hostage . . . knife point . . .'

Hastening to reach the platform, Carolides wasted no niceties on the passengers blocking his path: 'Out of my way!' he shouted at their startled faces. They fumbled to step aside, letting him and his hostage through. This time, when the girl summoned the courage to scream again, there were fewer passengers and less noise than there had been at the barrier, and the sound of her cry brought immediate attention. Hoping to lose his pursuers, Carolides ran towards the end of the platform, away from the staircase and towards the labyrinthine underground railyards. Then he paused, out of breath. His grip still firm, he clutched the girl and his briefcase even more tightly. Some passengers on the platform scrambled to get out of the way; others, paralysed by panic, froze in their tracks.

Only a few yards down the line from Carolides, in the shadow of a station support and out of the Cuban terrorist's line of vision, a man wearing a beige suit and black leather gloves calmly withdrew a silencer from his pocket and screwed it on his gun. From behind him, he could feel the rumbling and hear the approach of the train entering the station. The engine's headlight flooded the post with a white light. The man, a tall, sturdy figure with chiselled features, was silhouetted in the light as he stepped from behind the pillar.

From the top of the staircase, the trio of agents, Anson, Hellman, and Mason, spotted Carolides and the girl. Hurtling over spilled packages and luggage, they raced down the steps which remained obstructed by the panicked passengers. Simultaneously, the stranger with the silencer stepped into the clear light of the station platform. The train whistle blew. Carolides whirled around to confront the stranger. As soon as he glimpsed the stranger's nearly white grey hair, the stranger ceased to be a stranger; immediately he recognized the chilling, tranquil presence before him as Robert McCall – respected, feared, admired,

11

and known in the Intelligence community as the 'Equalizer'.

At the sight of McCall, who stepped fearlessly towards him, Carolides dragged the girl a few steps away, He shrieked, his voice becoming suddenly high-pitched and breaking. 'I'll cut her throat.'

The Equalizer maintained his calm demeanour and stared at Carolides with an unnerving intensity. His gun remained at his side. McCall's firm, gentle voice and distinct British accent bespoke authority. 'Let her go,' he commanded the terrorist. 'It's over, Carolides. Just you and I. The way it should be.'

Carolides paused. The petrified girl in his vice-like grip whimpered. The train was a silver streak as it zipped by, slowed, and then braked to a screeching halt. The passengers waiting on the platform withdrew from the two men and the girl, clearing back to the side opposite the train.

'What's in the briefcase isn't worth your life,' McCall explained quietly. 'Let her go.'

The girl began to cry and tremble violently, squeezing her eyes shut as if to block out the danger. Then she felt her captor's grasp relax, and the next thing she knew he shoved her aside. Caught off guard by her unexpected release, she stumbled to her knees. She watched as Carolides – now himself a hostage of the Equalizer – began to shake, his strained Cuban face finally coming unglued and dissolving into tears. Like a scolded child, he raised the briefcase and extended it, a peace offering, toward the Equalizer.

At the other end of the platform, Mason, on reaching the bottom of the staircase, saw the girl fall away from Carolides. The Cuban was now an open target, his back turned towards the agent. This was exactly the kind of break Mason had been waiting for. His gun already in hand, he raised it, aimed, and fired. The shot sounded like a muffled firecracker. It struck Carolides in the back.

McCall saw Carolides, a quizzical look on his face, stagger forward before he dropped the briefcase, then swerved around, and grabbed the girl's shoulder. Again, his knife was raised, and it was clear to McCall that the Cuban's last act was to be to drive the blade into his hostage. Firing from the hip, McCall caught Carolides with a second bullet. Stunned, the terrorist dropped the knife and slumped into a heap on the platform. A cloud of smoke wafted past McCall's impassive face as he moved towards the hysterical girl. No longer certain who the enemy was, she scooted away from the body where a pool of blood was collecting, then away from McCall.

The doors of the train jerked open. Most of the arriving passengers failed to notice the bizarre tableau near the end of the platform. The transfixed crowd of witnesses which clustered around the death scene began to stir again, some of them hastening onto the train for seats, others hanging back to gawk at the violence. Mason's gun was still brandished as he and his fellow agents Hellman and Anson ran up to survey the body. Carolides lay face up, the blood from the two bullet holes in his back spilling out from underneath him. It was obvious he was dead; nonetheless, Anson stooped down and took Carolides' hand and felt for a pulse. It came as no great surprise that there wasn't one. Hellman snatched the precious briefcase. Pleased with himself, Mason gloried in the moment and gloated over the corpse as if it were game he had bagged on safari.

'I got him first,' he boasted smugly to fellow agent McCall.

It wasn't just the shine in Mason's eyes that disturbed McCall. It was the dead young man lying before him, the sobbing girl, and the heartless audacity of his brother agents standing across from him. Without saying a word, he casually raised his gun again. A look of terror swept across Mason's face as he stared down the long, dark gun silencer and barrel. After holding the gun in position for a moment, McCall suddenly lowered it, slipped it back inside his jacket, and walked down the echoing platform, disappearing into the anonymous throng of departing, shocked passengers.

13

TWO

A short time ago – in the days before he became popularly known about New York as the Equalizer – McCall walked out on the likes of Mason, Hellman, and Anson. His career with the Agency ended abruptly, not because of one particular incident like the one in Grand Central, but as a result of a succession of events and forces piling up over the years, taking their toll on his emotions, eroding his belief in his profession, infringing on his personal life. McCall was still a good agent at the peak of his form. Some said the best. The Agency wasn't prepared to lose him. Had he bothered to enquire first (which he didn't), he would have learned that retirement wasn't even an option open to company operatives. Whether it was a policy of retirement or some other Agency edict, McCall, a man of deep intregrity, only showed respect for policies worth respecting. Gradually, with an oppressive sadness, he had come to realize that somehow things in the company had gone askew. Or maybe he had changed, and with the change his perspective had shifted. Whatever the case, he had no choice but to do things his way.

And so it was that he was full of resolve that muggy summer Washington day when he drove the short distance from his Georgetown home to the Agency headquarters in Virginia and faced his colleagues, as one of them, for the last time. He was certain they would try to talk him out of retiring. They would probably cajole him at first; then would come the expressions of concern, perhaps followed by flattery and, as a last resort, coercion. But McCall hadn't been prepared for the hostility confronting him in the cold, oversized government conference room. It had never appeared so large or so drained of colour before. The faces around him were ashen. The white walls were stark. The bleached wood in the circular table took on the hue of stone. The huge operations map with its rainbow of push pins provided the only bare trace of colour and life in the room.

His fellow operatives, gathered around the large circular table, had listened attentively to McCall's assessment of the Agency, his view of his role in it, and his objections to the way in which it had come to do business of late. None of his remarks in and of themselves was particularly startling to these men. McCall was always a man to speak his mind. In fact, all but one of the Agency men reacted to his remarks with controlled silence. The exception was Brahms, a heavy, wise-cracking, balding, perpetually rebellious operative – the 'bad boy' of Operations. He paced and fidgeted as McCall's 'Control' – an elegant, articulate, Yale-educated black man – rose and delivered a rebuttal to McCall's arguments. As usual Brahms showed little reverence for Control in declaring that he was on McCall's side. The heated discussion prompted McCall to explode in a sudden rage as he let it be loudly known that he had made his decision about the Agency. There were more words exchanged, then McCall hurled his prepared letter of resignation on the table and strode out of the room. The last thing he heard as the door closed behind him was the dull, rhythmic slap of Brahms' applauding hands.

*   *   *

15

McCall could criticize the Agency on several counts, but one thing was true: it had always paid well. And that money had now bought him a spacious New York co-op on a brownstone block in the fashionable East Fifties. McCall intended to make a home again for himself, in Manhattan, near his former wife and son. It had been ten years since he had known a real home. They were in California then – he, Janice, and Scott. Scott had grown up in Santa Monica near a small park. Their home was small and cheap, but living there had been the happiest years of McCall's life. That was before his work got in the way. Years slipped by, and he was away a lot of the time on business trips to exotic, faraway places on missions he could never discuss with his family. Janice and Scott, involved in their own lives apart from his, receded into the distance until the emotional fabric and common activities which held them together as a family dissolved. Divorce followed. They agreed that Janice would raise Scott; it would only be proper since McCall didn't have the time to be a devoted father. Janice decided to move East. She wanted to start fresh, with no familiar walls and their memories to frame her life. McCall moved to Washington, a good idea, he thought, so he could be closer to headquarters – and forget more readily what he'd left behind.

Now on a brisk November day, he returned to the New York neighbourhood where he'd always dreamed of living with Scott and Janice. The fantasy had never died. Standing on the sidewalk by the moving van, he supervised the movers as they unloaded his furniture from the truck. A man facing an exciting new life, McCall wandered through the empty white rooms, his contentment fighting an occasional wave of nostalgia. As the movers carted his modern furniture, crates and paintings up the steps, he rejoiced in his new-found freedom by directing the traffic through the house.

Before nightfall all the furniture was in place. Boxes were piled everywhere. Most of them remained unopened, although McCall had hastily unpacked some of them, pulling out an array of books and office supplies. Scott and Janice's pictures already sat on the empty mantelpiece in the cosy study. Sitting down behind the typewriter at his desk, McCall completed the first order of business of his new life by composing an ad to appear in the New York *Times*.

The day the ad was published, an early snow fell unexpectedly on the city, turning McCall's quaint, tree-lined block of townhouses into a beautifully pristine landscape. McCall revelled in the falling snow. The wizened vendor at the corner news-stand grumbled about having to cover his papers. Laughing and slapping the vendor on the back good-naturedly, McCall handed him the coins for the *Times*, then stood there and flipped to the classifieds. Leaping out boldly at him from a box were his words:

GOTTA PROBLEM? ODDS AGAINST YOU? CALL THE EQUALIZER.

He felt a warm glow go through his body and smiled, satisfied, as the snow flakes softly lighted on his grey hair. At last his life had what it had lacked for too long – a sense of purpose, and the certain knowledge that this time around he would make a difference on behalf of justice, decency, and the good of his fellow man.

The Equalizer, he said aloud to himself. Brahms started calling him that. He'd never worn the name comfortably, but . . . yes, now it had a nice ring to it, he thought.

THREE

Bill Hamilton had a problem, though it wasn't the type of problem requiring the services of the Equalizer, at least not yet. Like hundreds of others on the floor of his company, Bill Hamilton, a computer drone in his ten by ten office cell, hacked away at his keyboard for the benefit of Metropolitan Telephone. His rumpled hair and smudged, horn-rimmed glasses gave Hamilton the look of a friendly nerd, which he was. Every morning he dreaded the glance in the mirror at the receding sandy hair and his athlete's body going to fat. Then there was the matter of his skin, which he swore to his wife, was turning green from over exposure to the fluorescent lighting. If he only had more hours in the day, he could get to the gym, maybe sign up for that special at the tanning centre . . . but there was never enough time. Hamilton would spend the rest of his life squirrelled away in the glass cage of the phone company office tower. His eyes riveted to the green phosphors of a computer screen, he'd long ceased to notice the magnificent view of the mid-town skyline outside his window.

Although it was only five o'clock, Hamilton knew this was going to be another late night. His co-workers in the rows of desks surrounding him were wiping clean their screens and heading home. But Hamilton continued to punch the keys like an attacker. Every time it was the same frustrating, dead-end result. The number 0900 would appear.

'There it is again,' he groaned to himself. 'This is crazy.'

His fingers flew across the board, punching up a new sentence command: *DISPLAY ACCOUNT No 0900*. He waited a beat only to have the words *SYNTAX ERROR* appear on the screen. Another command wiped the screen clean so that he could give it one more go with a series of new numbers. But on every series he tried, long rows of them, the number 0900 continued to appear on each list.

Sherry had been sympathetic to Hamilton's 0900 problem ever since it began a few days ago; now it was starting to grate on her nerves as well as his. She could tell by the determined, fretful look on her co-worker's face that he would be camping out at the office half the night unless he found a solution to the 0900 menace. Moving past his desk, she glanced down at the screen to confirm her suspicions.

'Can't you leave it alone, Bill?' she asked as she stacked some files away in a drawer. 'It's a number buried with lots of other numbers. Go home to your wife and throw the telephone out the window.'

Hamilton ran his fingers through his thinning hair, heaved a sigh, and pleaded for more support. 'That number shouldn't be there,' he maintained. 'It doesn't correlate to any of my charts. If it's a frozen account it wouldn't show up in the binary numbers.' Sherry wearily shrugged her shoulders. 'It doesn't exist,' he shrieked, 'but it's *there!*'

'Who cares?' Sherry asked, pleading with him. 'This is becoming an obsession with you.' She punched him playfully in the arm. 'Lighten up. I'll see you next door for a beer.'

Vaguely, Hamilton waved an acknowledgement, his eyes still transfixed to the screen. Convinced her friend was becoming a cipher zombie, Sherry gathered her pocketbook and walked to the elevator bank. As she waited for the elevator, she could see him punching more keys, calling up more sets of rotating numbers on the glowing green screen, slamming his fist against the desk in exasperation. Some guys just didn't know when to quit.

Farther uptown, on Manhattan's trendy Upper West Side, the bright crimson rays of the sun setting across the Hudson worked their way through the crosstown streets, cast long shadows across the avenues, and caught the tops of old brick apartment buildings and Central Park West's art deco spires. At times like these New York basked in the Dutch light of old Flemish masters. In the quiet residential streets with their rows of renovated brownstones, the sound of traffic disappeared for the most part, and conversations, operatic voices practising arias, or the sound of children at play floated through the air.

In a school yard a short distance from the boutiques and restaurants of Columbus Avenue, children tossed balls, crawled through barrels, and climbed up slides while their parents, arriving on foot and by car, picked them up to take them home. Colleen Randall arrived late in her dented blue Ford to collect her nine-year-old daughter, Sarah. She wouldn't bother to look for a parking space this afternoon, since the odds against finding one were overwhelmingly against her; so she double-parked by the playground like everyone else.

As she parked the car, she glanced about for Sarah but couldn't find her daughter, who looked remarkably like a pint-sized model of her. In her late thirties, Colleen still had naturally bright red hair, a clear complexion, vibrant green eyes, and a dancer's body, all of which made her look at least ten years younger. Jogging down the sidewalk in her track suit, she could easily have been mistaken for one of the neighbourhood's regular runners. She was jogging up to the schoolyard gate when she spotted Sarah.

Her daughter, who appeared to Colleen to be terrified, was cowering against the fence, backing away from a young man who wore jeans and an Army fatigue coat. Colleen couldn't tell from her perspective whether or not he was a neighbourhood street tough, but his wild curly hair and the large sheathed hunting knife dangling from his belt gave him the look of a Third World revolutionary, giving Colleen reason enough to be alarmed. After apparently berating Sarah, the young man smiled and laid a reassuring hand on her shoulder. Sarah may have been reassured; her mother wasn't.

'Sarah . . .' Colleen cried out over the din of the children's voices in the school yard.

Spotting her mother across the obstacle course that was the playground, Sarah pushed off the fence to run past the stranger, who impulsively ruffled her hair. Sarah shoved her way between the other kids to get to her mum. Although Sarah was running away from the young man and couldn't see him, Colleen watched as he turned, flashed Sarah an unnatural grin, then walked out of sight behind the building. When Sarah reached her, Colleen stooped down, took her daughter in her arms, and hugged her tightly.

'I've told you not to talk to strangers,' she said, gently admonishing Sarah. 'What did he say to you?'

Usually effervescent, Sarah, feeling guilty, became suddenly shy. 'We were talking about *Sesame Street*. He's very nice.' Suddenly Sarah's face brightened and, in hopes of pleasing her mother, she added hastily, 'He likes your hair. He says it tumbles on your shoulders and is very beautiful.'

Colleen's face tightened with distress. Instinctively, she pulled Sarah closer to her, as though shielding her from harm. 'Never mind what he said, Sarah. You must promise me you'll never speak to him again.' Sarah's small face resumed its glum expression. Colleen tilted her daughter's chin up with her hand and looked her directly in the eye. 'And if you see him here, you go directly to one of the teachers.' Colleen extended her hand to Sarah. 'We gotta deal, kid?'

The two of them solemnly shook on it. Taking Sarah in hand, Colleen briskly walked her through the crowded playgroup to the car. As Colleen opened the door for Sarah, she failed to notice the young man who had reappeared beside another section of fence from which he could surreptitiously spy on mother and daughter. Intent on staring at Colleen, he unconsciously unwrapped a candy bar, all the while smiling and humming softly to himself. As they pulled away in the blue Ford, he noted the car and its licence plate and, very satisfied with himself, broke off a big bite of the candy with his teeth.

He knew they'd be back . . . and so would he.

FOUR

By night its massive dark stones and heavy architectural design gave the building on West 44th Street the look of a foreboding German fortress which was completely out of keeping with the Bauhaus insurance skyscraper across the street on Sixth Avenue. Only the warm glow of yellow lights through the windows made the High School of Performing Arts more welcoming that the Bastille. There were no apparent signs indicating that this institution, part of the City of New York's specialized high school system, was responsible for turning out some of the arts' most brilliant young performers in the fields of music, dance, singing, and acting. From here, it was only a short jump to Broadway – a proximity which inspired some of its young students, and made others all that more impatient to get there.

When he stepped through the double-door entrance to the school, the Equalizer felt suddenly out of place here, not only because the building was foreign to him, but because he was surrounded by teenagers. Dressed in an overcoat and conservative suit, McCall was momentarily overwhelmed by the energy of youth swirling about him. Kids, carrying props for scenes, ran through halls. Others bustled past with armloads of books. He saw more than one music student hurrying by – two with guitars, one with a violin, another sorting through disorganized pages of sheet music. McCall laughed to himself. His tall, striking figure must have appeared to these kids as a pillar of authority. All of them, even those who were curious, did their best to ignore his presence. Not knowing where to turn in the long corridor, the Equalizer finally caught the arm of a girl walking by.

'Excuse me,' he asked her, 'where's the rehearsal?'

'Which one?' she laughed. McCall studied her face. It was one of those radiant young, slightly off-centred beautiful faces brimming with enthusiasm. Her voice trilled with a natural theatrical quality. 'We've got *Taming of the Shrew* in room six, *The Rainmaker* in nine, and Tom Stoppard's *The Real Thing* – just the cricket-bat scene – in room twelve.'

'The music rehearsal,' McCall explained.

She looked at his bemused blue eyes and giggled. 'Guess you figured out I'm not the music type, huh? Wonder what gave it away? You a cop or something?'

'Right now I'm trying to be a father.'

'Good luck at it,' she teased. 'Auditorium's right around the corner. It's almost over, though. You're late,' she said, then started on down the hall, spun around, and added, 'but you're real cute.'

'Better late than never . . .' McCall began, his words trailing off as the girl flew out of sight before he had a chance to finish. Had he heard her correctly? 'Cute,' she'd said. Feeling suddenly more her age than his, he moved down the hallway towards the auditorium.

McCall quietly entered the small rehearsal hall, the stirring sounds of Beethoven's Fifth Symphony rousing him as he slid into a seat in the darkened rear of the room. The school orchestra clustered together on stage while the music teacher, Marvin Einhorn, a charismatic, European conductor of the old school of gentleman maestros, immersed himself with a passion into the score. Except for McCall and a handful of music students scattered through the seats, there was no audience to enjoy the strains of the uplifting final movement. McCall leaned forward towards the empty row ahead of him and gazed profoundly at his son.

The first violinist, Scott, moved the bow across the strings with enthusiasm. McCall knew how much his son adored Beethoven, but he was amazed he could do justice to the complex score with all its subtleties. Though Scott was nearly his father's height, McCall continued to see in his mind's eye the little boy scratching away at a fiddle on the beach in Santa Monica. With his blond hair, blue eyes, and lean surfer good looks, Scott still seemed as if he ought to be on a California beach, or a 'Guys of Southern California Calender', not a concert stage.

Scott carried his handsomeness confidently, without arrogance, having inherited his father's sense of assurance along with his intelligence. At least McCall had given his son that. His chin resting on his hands as he leaned forward on the seat in front of him, the Equalizer was transfixed by Scott's intense eyes, and, as he heard him play with an intensity to match their sparkle, only wished he had the joy they gave off to the audience. A distant memory, joy. Joy was something McCall had misplaced somewhere along the path leading out of his too-brief youth.

Engrossed by the music and his memories, McCall jumped at the sound of conductor Einhorn's baton rapping the music stand in front of him. McCall wondered why. To his ear, the music was magnificently performed. Obviously, Mr Einhorn had a different opinion. The last notes of the orchestra faded away and the musicians put down their instruments and met their teacher's gaze. Mr Einhorn stood woefully shaking his head like an exasperated parent whose supply of patience had been exhausted.

'I have many conflicting emotions,' Mr Einhorn told them. 'Pride, exhilaration, patience, understanding, and a tin ear would help.' A titter of laughter ripped through the orchestra until the teacher jabbed the air with his baton, pointing out individuals. 'Mr McCall,' he began, motioning to Scott, who listened attentively, 'that is a violin you are sawing on, not a leg of lamb.' McCall nearly rose from his seat to lodge a protest, but thought better of it when he realized this was a school, not an Agency conference room. The conductor's tone became more sarcastic. 'Mr Picollo, what has the oboe ever done to you?' There was no more laughter as each of the musicians waited for the axe to fall on him next. 'Miss Jenkins, I know when you're faking it.' She started to protest and he cut her off with, 'Save that for your boyfriend.' Putting his baton down, he gathered up his score and walked off the podium. 'Rehearsal tomorrow afternoon at three.'

The orchestra broke up, the young musicians quickly packing their instruments away. McCall rose from his seat and headed down the side aisle towards the front of the auditorium. He caught Scott just as his son was jumping down off the stage with his violin case in his hand.

'Sounded pretty good to me . . .'

Still in something of an emotional fog, Scott was jarred by the unexpected sound of his father's voice. 'Well, hello there,' he said, with some awkwardness and suppressed anger. 'It's been a long time.'

'Too long, Scott . . .' McCall offered gently as an apology, laying his hand on his son's shoulder.

'Still remember my name?' said Scott, abruptly moving away. 'Good start.'

The Equilizer followed Scott down the aisle towards the back of the auditorium.

'I deserve that.'

Scott, confused by a mass of conflicting feelings, shook his head. 'No, you don't. It's just a long time since you've been to a concert.'

'I'm going to have a lot more time to do the things I've wanted to.'

'That's nice,' Scott said, but he really didn't know what to say. He wanted to say the right thing, but he wasn't sure just what the right thing was for an eighteen-year-old kid

26

who missed his father more than he would let on. 'You're looking good. When *was* the last time? Christmas? New Year's . . .' Scott shrugged; it really didn't matter when it was. What mattered is that it had been so long he couldn't remember. 'Some holiday. You'd just come back from one of those ravaged countries. A takeover. I watched it on the news. Fifteen Americans killed, but someone got a whole bunch of college kids to the airport in a commandeered, battered old school bus. I always wondered if that was you.' The Equalizer's cool eyes didn't admit to anything. 'Was it?'

'It might have been.'

Damn, every time he felt himself getting close to his father, Dad closed up again. Things weren't any different and they weren't going to be. Scott had nothing further to say to a father who wouldn't answer one question from his son which meant something. Had he stopped being a father for so long that he couldn't see when his own son wanted him to be a hero for him?

As Scott walked silently past his father toward the lighted exit sign, he felt the Equalizer's hand around his arm and stopped cold. The other student musicians hurried past, giving Scott odd glances and wondering if he might be in trouble.

'I've resigned,' McCall told his son.

Scott stared at his father, not quite believing the news. 'I didn't think you were allowed to do that.'

'You're allowed to follow the course you believe in.'

'That's what you've been doing all these years?' Scott caught himself as the anger finally bubbled to the surface and shot out like a dagger. God, he felt awful about it, but the words were already out, the damage done. 'Lousy thing to say,' he explained himself, trying to smooth over it. McCall nodded. '"Shadow Man." That's what my friends always called you. "The phantom." "Where's your dad, Scott? How come he only visits one weekend a month? What does he *really* do? You can tell us. He's in the mob? The government? How come he abandoned you?"' Suddenly Scott laughed loud enough to fill the emptying auditorium.

'I popped the last guy who said that. Like father, like son . . .'

'Maybe we can both learn to control some emotions.'

'It isn't too late?'

'Not for me.'

'Then I guess it can't be too late for me.'

McCall relaxed at the gentler tone of Scott's words. The days you're talking about are gone. New slate. Feels good.'

Scott sensed an inner peace coming from his father. Maybe things would be different, after all. The man standing before him was more than calm. There was another aura about his father which Scott had never seen in him before.

'So what are you going to do with this "new slate?"'

'Step back,' responded the Equalizer. 'Look around. Get to know my son a little better.'

Scott grinned boyishly at his father. 'Better talk to your ex-wife about that. She's pretty independent now. She's got a good job, friends, new photos on the mantelpiece, a charge card at Bloomies that's all paid up. She feels pretty good about herself. You can't spoil that.'

'Maybe I can enhance it.'

'Not unless you've changed an awful lot,' replied Scott softly, hesitant to burst his father's bubble, but needing to make him aware of the realities of the situation.

'I'd like to prove that to both of you.'

Doubtful, Scott was still willing to give his father that chance. 'You know where to find me.' He glanced anxiously at his watch. 'Look, I've got four hours of practice before old maestro Einhorn breaks my violin bow over his knee.' Without going through the awkward formality of shaking hands, or the unfathomable intimacy of hugging, Scott turned to go and headed up the aisle. While he didn't want to be hurt again by feelings of abandonment, neither did he want to shut his father out of his life. Turning back towards him, he extended an invitation to keep the door open. 'If you're going to be in town a while, we put this thing together in a couple of nights.'

'I'll be there,' the Equalizer told his son. 'That's a promise.'

'I'll be looking for you.' He started off again then, brightening, turned back. 'It's great to see you, Dad. It really is.'

'Likewise.'

Searching for the right words, he spoke again, his voice softer. 'I've always hoped you were the one driving that school bus.'

McCall wanted so much to say he was the one just to please his son, but his face didn't betray his restraint or his feelings until Scott exited into the hallway; only then did the Equalizer finally smile.

FIVE

When the Equalizer asked his former wife Janice to meet
him at the skating rink at Rockefeller Center, he wasn't
sure she would even show up. Neither was she until the last
minute. He spotted her in the plaza as she approached,
wrapped in a black fur coat, walking down the arcade
through the throngs of tourists. She appeared more elegant
than he remembered her. The harsh floodlights which lit
the cluster of Depression Era skyscrapers did nothing to
diminish the loveliness of her face. Admiring her from a
short distance, the Equalizer remained at the railing above
the skating rink.. Janice seemed out of breath when she
finally stood before him, and both of them, like school kids
on a first date, hesitated before embracing. McCall kissed
her lightly and hugged her as though he'd never let go. It
was too much for her. She was overwhelmed by her feelings
and wasn't prepared for so powerful a gesture of affection.
She turned away from him and looked down at the skaters
circling the ice below. Sensing something was amiss,
McCall gave her the opening to offer an explanation.

'I really debated meeting you tonight. But you saw Scott. That's not something you would do without a reason.'

'I've told you the reason . . .'

Suddenly Janice didn't want to hear any more. Maybe this rendezvous was a bad idea. What had she hoped to gain from it anyway? Was she being nostalgic? Was she punishing herself? If only there were an easy, simple explanation. She knew Robert wanted this reunion more than she did and, like it or not, she was going to have to listen to him state his case. Already he was moving after her as she stepped away from him.

It was at that moment the shadow assassin came out of nowhere.

Although Janice sensed a stranger stumbling towards them at the railing, she thought little of it. She was accustomed to being jostled on the city's sidewalks and subways, and there was nothing about the compactly built man to make her suspicious. But the Equalizer's guard went up the instant the man, who had been observing them for several moments, put his hand on McCall's shoulder by way of an apology. No sooner had the short, wiry stranger mumbled the apology, than McCall saw the glint of the knife flashing. Whirling around suddenly, the Equalizer sprang into action. Before the assassin could react, McCall clamped a hand over his knife hand, swung the man around and up onto the railing, and twisted his wrist until the pain forced him to drop the knife. It fell to the rink below, clattering on the ice where a skater swerved, narrowly avoiding it. If McCall chose to let go, the assassin would follow his knife to the ice two storeys below.

Janice wasn't aware of the grave danger until she saw the knife fall and McCall holding the stranger over the edge of the wall. Her hand flew to her mouth to stifle a scream. Simultaneously, the bystanders in the immediate vicinity pulled back out of the way, leaving a wide berth between them and the two men. It was clear to the witnesses that the older, distinguished man with the grey hair had the advantage. With one hand, he gripped the smaller man tightly by the lapel to keep him from falling, and with the other he pressed the man's throat back.

The coolness in McCall's voice belied the inherent violence of the situation. 'Any reason you can think of why I don't just let go?' The horrified assassin stared bug-eyed at the Equalizer. 'Tell Control not to send anyone else,' the Equalizer continued. 'I might not be in such a charitable mood next time.'

The would-be assassin was speechless as the Equalizer hauled him back from the brink of the railing. Meanwhile a pair of uniformed cops ran through the crowd to reach the source of the commotion. Before they arrived, McCall thrust the assassin to his knees on the pavement and left him there for the police. Unflustered, he walked over to Janice, whose tense body was still recoiling from the shock of the attack. Taking her in gentlemanly fashion by the arm, he propelled her swiftly away from the skating rink. The crowd of witnesses, anxious to tell their stories to the police, closed in on the quaking assailant, preventing his escape.

The Equalizer and Janice had reached Fifth Avenue before she composed herself enough to speak.

'Who was that?' she asked.

'Doesn't matter.'

Years of anger intensified by incident welled up from inside. 'So laconic. So calm. Of *course* it matters! Someone just tried to kill you! What little hot spot in the world are you trying to cool down this time? What enemy agent wants you dead?'

'I've resigned,' he stated simply. 'That's what I wanted to tell you tonight.'

'Maybe you should inform the "other side" – whoever the hell they are. Or is it your own side?'

The sarcasm cut deep. 'Janice . . .'

In front of Sak's Fifth Avenue amid the crush of shoppers, Janice came to a sudden halt on the middle of the sidewalk and held her ground.

'Stay away from me, Robert,' she warned him softly but

firmly. 'Stay away from our son. No stray bullets. Let him live his life. Let me live mine. However lonely it is without you.' Abruptly, she turned and walked away without so much as a look or a word of good-bye.

He hadn't expected it to end like this. So soon. So unresolved. She didn't bother to glance back or linger – not even for the moment it would have taken for her to read the pain and frustration in the Equalizer's eyes.

That was the day Bill Hamilton contemplated the odd ad in the classifieds again. He'd been checking it every day for the past week – ever since he lost his job at the phone company. Now that someone had tried to run him off the road on his way home to New Bedford, Connecticut, maybe he ought to try the number and see what happened. Who was this Equalizer character? He felt silly even thinking of calling the guy. It sounded about as ridiculous as phoning up Superman and asking him to hop into the nearest phone booth and fly right over. But Hamilton was at the end of his tether. The 0900 menace had been causing him sleepless nights and ruining his days at the phone company for weeks. His work pal Sherry had barely spoken to him his last few days there, and the other workers shunned him as if he were an outcast. Hamilton had imagined a lot of scenarios; being fired was not one of them. But a week ago it had happened, without further explanation. One day a marketing wizard; the next day on the street. Making the mortgage payments and supporting his kids in boarding school had now taken a back seat to his basic survival instincts. He didn't think this Equalizer could get him his job back. Right now, that wasn't the greatest of his worries.

At home in New Bedford with his wife Ellen, Hamilton tried to calm himself enough to take action. His desk reflected his state of disarray. Books and papers were haphazardly opened and strewn about. In front of him, the newspaper was opened to the classifieds, the Equalizer's ad circled in red ink. Looking older than her forty-three years, Ellen's face was drawn with fear and anxiety. The crow's feet around her eyes were more pronounced. Hamilton thought there was even more grey in her brown hair than the day before. Wringing her hands, she paced and looked out the second-storey window behind Hamilton's desk. In the glow of the streetlamp, she could see the first flakes of a falling night snow. While she fretted, her husband's hand still cradled the receiver, his index finger holding down the receiver button as he tried to muster the nerve to call for help.

'Call the police,' Ellen pleaded.

'And tell them what?' Hamilton asked. 'That I was fired from my job at the telephone company after twenty-two years? That some maniac tried to run me off the road, and that I'm sure the two things are connected.' He put the handset back in the cradle and pushed the phone away from him.

'But *why*?'

'I found something I wasn't looking for. Something no one else could've found.'

'What?'

He leaned back in his chair and took a deep breath. 'I'm not sure. A code. I dialled one of the numbers in it. I got through to the Pentagon.'

'Is that why someone tried to kill you?'

Baffled, Hamilton shook his head. 'I don't know.'

'Well, we've got to do something,' insisted Helen. 'The kids will be back home this weekend. There's got to be someone you can call. A private detective. Someone . . .'

Hamilton picked up the newspaper with the circled ad.

'Been noticing this for the last week,' he said, then read it to her. '"Gotta problem? Odds against you? Call the Equalizer."'

Ellen looked at her husband with a blank, perplexed expression. 'What does it mean?'

'I'm not sure,' he said, thinking for a moment before reaching for the phone. Ellen was right. They couldn't endanger the kids. Best to do something before it was too late. It was about time he made that call.

SIX

The Equalizer looked up from the liver cooking in the sauté pan and saw the snow falling outside the large living room windows. There was something soothing about the snow, particularly after the strained conversation he'd had with Janice and the incident with the assassin. The assassin was something he had dealt with all his working life, an occupational hazard as it were. The rift between him and his family was more difficult to deal with, though he often tried to rationalize to make himself feel better. For a man who couldn't afford guilt in his line of work, McCall was feeling more than his share of it. How many times had people told him he was 'only human?' Sometimes he'd wondered about that as well.

Cooking in his new modern kitchen pleased him. The entire apartment had that effect on him. It was something like a new toy for an overgrown kid; perhaps Janice was not far from the truth when she accused him of being emotionally immature. But little things like plumbing that worked and an oven which cleaned itself counted for a lot in a complicated world. Things gave him a certain amount of pleasure.

McCall slid the liver out of the pan and into a dish, then carried it into the living room where his Irish setter eagerly awaited his dinner in front of the hearth. Stooping by the blazing fire, he petted the dog and set the liver in front of him. The dog devoured it instantly. McCall eased himself into an Eames chair by the window and poured a glass of whisky. He glanced around the living space he'd made and admired the end result. The eggshell tones of the walls blended perfectly with the soft pastels of his contemporary painting and impressionist oils. He had great pride in his collection, which had taken more than Agency money to assemble properly. In becoming an interior designer, Janice had picked up much of her impeccable taste from her husband, who had an eye for fine art and things of quality. The apartment's designer furnishings, even his gun collection, were museum quality. The rich Persian tapestry which covered the dark hardwood floor was a priceless rug which couldn't be bought anywhere – a token of gratitude from a member of the Shah's family whose life McCall had saved from the Khomeini revolution. The art gifts had made his mercenary work more rewarding, although they couldn't adequately compensate for its more gruelling aspects.

Staring into the fire, McCall wondered why human relationships had to be so difficult. Why couldn't a man simply make his feelings known and have those close to him accept and understand him? He'd made a point of not holding grudges in his life. Anger turned inward was an insidious poison. The healthiest thing people could do was to accept others, including their limitations, and get on with their own lives. The problem now was his need to involve those he loved in a life he'd excluded them from for so long. Loving them wasn't the hard part; it was fighting for his ideals at the same time that created the conflict. How he could resolve that conflict was a question he believed could be answered only by time and experience. If he were lucky,

Janice and Scott would give him the chance to prove himself.

The phone rang and startled him from his reflective moment.

'Yes?' he answered.

In his Connecticut study, Bill Hamilton cleared his throat. His voice quivered. 'My name is Hamilton,' he began hesitantly. 'I read your ad. I'm in trouble. Someone tried to kill me tonight.'

'I know the feeling,' the Equalizer commented wryly.

To McCall, the nervous voice on the other end of the line seemed eager to get all the information out in the open. 'I don't know who you are, but . . .'

'I'll meet you at the New York Café, overlooking the UN Building,' McCall interrupted him. 'Noon tomorrow,' he instructed. 'Sit at the last booth. Come alone.'

The Equalizer rang off, picked up his whisky glass, and drained it, then turned the Baccarat crystal over in his fingers.

'Have faith in me, Janice,' he said to her picture on the mantle. 'We're going to be together again . . . all I have to do is stay alive.'

While the Equalizer contemplated his future, and Bill Hamilton did his best to assure his wife Ellen that everything would be all right, two telephone company executives met secretly in Hamilton's former mid-town office building.

Their rendezvous took place in an office more intimate and elegant than the fluorescent-lit cube where Hamilton had toiled over a computer screen. The gilded nameplate on the huge mahogany desk read: *LEONARD MANETTI*. Manetti had fought to get to the top. He'd do anything to maintain the good life and the status symbolized by his office. Everything surrounding Manetti was in corporate good taste without reflecting any individual personality. The design was planned to impress rather than to convey an inviting quality. The wood panelling, red leather wing chairs, heavy drapes, and portrait gallery made Manetti feel as if he were in an exclusive men's club – which was his notion of having arrived at the top.

The only thing to indicate that this was a major corporation and not a university club was the map of the United States which covered one wall and showed the intricate telephone lines crisscrossing the continent. Manetti glanced up at the map, then went back to the computer terminal on his desk. A thin, powerful man with a hardened, Mediterranean face who almost always got what he wanted, Manetti had achieved his success in the communications world by the time he was forty. Now that he was nearly fifty and head of a powerful phone company division, the power had gone to his head. He considered himself above the rules of corporations and society, preferring to do what was best for himself rather than the good of the public. Punching in a code, he retrieved privileged data from the company's private files.

Sitting opposite Manetti was his associate Jim Olsen, an older, heavier man who moved and thought more slowly than Manetti.

'Who did Hamilton call?' Olsen asked.

'I'm finding out right now,' Manetti told him as he tapped the keyboard.

The name *ROBERT McCALL* flashed on the green screen, followed by the data: *McCALL SECURITY COMPANY. 348 E. 52ND STREET, NEW YORK, 10019.* Manetti's fingers continued to fly over the typewriter keys. Then the screen cleared and two new lines appeared: *McCALL SECURITY INC. LICENSED SECURITY COMPANY. BONDED 10/14/84.*

Though they'd gotten their data, Olsen and Manetti weren't especially happy with what it indicated – that Hamilton was getting professional help to deal with his 'problem'.

'Protection company,' Olsen grumbled. 'Bonded security officer. Now what do we do?'

'We'll handle it,' Manetti said.

38

The new revelation caused Olsen to pale as he realized the new risk they were taking. 'I can't be involved in any of this any longer. You said two months and we'd fold up. If any of the company directors discovered what we've . . .'

Manetti cut in, interrupting his associate. 'It's a closed cell. No one knows what we're doing.'

'Hamilton found out,' Olsen reminded his cohort.

'Twenty-four hours,' Manetti told him confidently. 'That's all we'll need to put the final squeeze on our Senator. Then we'll close the cell and start it up again in six months.'

'And Robert McCall?'

Manetti killed the light on the computer screen.

'I said we'd handle it . . .'

SEVEN

Although Colleen Randall was unaware of the Equalizer, she had come to wish constantly for some kind of white knight to rescue her from the current distress in her life. Fearful more for Sarah's sake than for her own, she didn't know where to turn. She had never been in this kind of trouble before. When her husband and she were living together she had always felt secure, and, after their divorce, she'd never felt any reason not to go on feeling that way – until now. An independent woman who worked as an art teacher, Colleen had grown to consider herself the strong, sensitive type. A lot of good that did her now, she thought to herself.

She hadn't actually seen the young man with the curly hair and Army fatigues since that day at the school yard. But that was little consolation. She had heard him. His phone calls had become a regular feature of terror and uncertainty in her life. Because she hadn't seen him, the anonymous calls were almost all the more ominous than if her tormentor made an appearance. She didn't know how he knew where she lived or who she was. Colleen had no idea how simple it was to trace a person from a New York licence plate if you paid the right people or had the right connections.

The young man cased her neighbourhood. Brushing the falling snow off his old leather bomber jacket, he pulled the black knit cap down over his head and made the phone call from a corner pay phone. Colleen lived on West 81st Street in an old rent-controlled apartment building. The phone booth was caddie-corner at the intersection of Amsterdam, just beside the mobbed yuppie grill which had opened to rave reviews and overflow singles crowds. As he dialled her number, the young man peered up into her lighted window and waited.

Inside her overheated, cramped apartment, Colleen had just stepped out of the shower when she heard the kitchen phone ringing. Sarah was sprawled on the living room floor where she was engrossed in *Magnum*. Absent-mindedly, she shovelled her dinner from a plate into her mouth. The ringing phone completely escaped her. She wouldn't have paid any attention to her mother if Colleen hadn't spoken to her as she ran into the kitchen and hastily tied a skimpy bathrobe around herself.

'Couldn't you answer the phone?' Colleen asked her.

'Not with Tom Magnum in this kind of trouble,' Sarah shot back without taking her eyes from a bare-chested Tom Selleck on the TV screen.

Making a face at Sarah, Colleen picked up the receiver. 'Hello?'

On the street below, the young man grew excited at the sound of Colleen's voice and began rattling off, in intimate, graphic detail, a long list of things he would like to do with Colleen's beautiful body. Colleen remained still, careful not to betray her emotions to Sarah. Silently, she began to cry. When she was certain that Sarah was still oblivious to her phone conversation, she crept farther into the small compact kitchen where her daughter would be less likely to hear her.

41

'Get your kicks, pal,' she said breaking in on his string of obscenities. 'Then I'm calling the police and . . .'

But he, being a pro who got his kicks from this sort of thing, had the upper hand on her.

'And tell them what, Colleen? My name is Steve, by the way. You've never asked, but I was sure you wanted to know. Secretly. Deep inside. I've so enjoyed our little phone conversations. But it's time to really meet. Don't you agree?'

Colleen felt herself losing her grip. 'Why . . . why are you doing this?'

'Because you're beautiful and I worship beauty. There's nothing wrong with that, is there?'

'Stop calling. Keep away from my daughter. The police will . . .'

'Do nothing, he laughed casually. 'You're never going to be rid of me, Colleen. Change your phone number, I'll find the new one. Move. I'll find you. I'm in your life now. I'll always be there. Part of you, Colleen.'

His smooth, sweet, almost musical voice aggravated her fear; finally, she couldn't tolerate any more and slammed down the phone. Her hand was still on the receiver when it began ringing again. She yanked the receiver off the hook, broke the connection, then left the handset lying on the kitchen counter. Drained, and feeling as if she'd been physically assaulted, she leaned against the counter, bracing herself.

The second phone call and Colleen's odd reaction had alerted Sarah that something was amiss. She took her attention from one of the TV show's frantic car chases and glanced over at her mother.

'What's the matter?'

'Nothing, honey,' Colleen told her, wiping her tears away quickly with the back of her hand. 'Eat your dinner and turn down the sound, please.'

Sarah obeyed Colleen's instructions and went back to her car chase; meanwhile, her mother hurried out of the living room into the hallway and checked the one lock on

42

the front door. After making sure it was secured, she returned to the living room.

The wind was rattling the glass in the window pane as the snow continued to come down. Colleen felt a draught and shivered. Her nerves on edge, she stared vacantly out the glass to the intersection at Amsterdam. There was a man in the phone booth looking up at her. Startled, she pulled her robe more tightly across her chest. The man grinned broadly, then pulled his knit cap off and waved it at her. Now there was no question it was the man from the school yard taunting her, and virtually on her doorstep. He disappeared around the corner. At least he hadn't come into the building. A momentary wave of relief swept through her. But when Colleen looked down at her hands, she caught her clenched fists banging against the glass.

EIGHT

'I don't believe it! Robert McCall! We've missed you!'

At the sight of the Equalizer entering the room, the blonde bartender, Carol, a Broadway and soap opera actress in her thirties, finished mixing a drink and abandoned her station behind the bar to greet her old friend. Carol and McCall had shared many late-night conversations over the bar at the New York Café Restaurant. That seemed like a long time ago. She was surprised to see him back in town.

'How are you doing?'

'Fine,' McCall nodded cheerfully, glancing around the restaurant. Though the food was elegant and the prices high, the New York Café always felt like home. Its proprietor, former chorus boy John Perry, never made it big on the Broadway stage, but his restaurant was a long-running hit on the shores of the East River. Boasting a magnificent view of the United Nations Building across the way, the restaurant was a special home to theatre people who yearned for a quiet evening of dining. As a homage to his

Broadway days, John Perry decorated the walls with theatrical touches: posters of plays, Hershfeld caricatures of stage personalities, photos of the good old days. With his dapper personal style and slicked-back hair, Perry himself was an anachronism.

'And how are you, Carol?' McCall greeted her with a warm handshake and a peck on the cheek. 'Any hot shows in town I should see?'

She pointed out the recent crop of theatre posters. 'Take your pick.' Giving his hand a squeeze, she headed back to the bar. 'Here's the boss. Don't go far.'

McCall smiled at her as the café's famed proprietor, John Perry, still looking like a slim and trim dancer in his late forties, strode quickly across the floor to welcome him back. Perry moved with the grace and ease of a kid hoofer. There were more lines around his eyes, but they still brimmed with youthful exuberance. The Equalizer couldn't recall if he had ever seen Perry when he wasn't smiling, or wearing a white suit with a red rose in his lapel.

Perry greeted him effusively in his dramatic tenor voice. 'Am I seeing things?'

'Broadway treating you well?' McCall asked, extending his hand.

'Ex-hoofers who go all the way back to *Top Banana* don't get many calls for *A Chorus Line*,' Perry laughed. 'But one of these days my style of dancing will return.'

'I hope so.'

Perry smiled. 'It's good to see you again. It's been too long.'

'Yes, it has. Get used to seeing me. I'm going to be around for a while.'

Perry, who knew something of McCall's line of work when he operated in New York for the Agency, had often kept his ears open for valuable information in the past. Perry's strategic location across the street from the international community of the UN made his café the favourite haunt of many diplomats and intelligence operatives such as McCall. Government secrets were swapped across these tables almost as frequently as show biz talk.

'No more missions?' Perry whispered to his old friend.

'Different ones.'

Perry surmised as much. 'A gentleman's waiting for you at the last booth. He looks scared.'

The Equalizer nodded and moved to the rear of the room without acknowledging Perry's 'Welcome home, Mr McCall.'

Just as the Equalizer expected, Hamilton was waiting for him in the appointed booth at the appointed time. Appraising Hamilton's nature by his clothes and demeanour as he approached the table, McCall had a sense of the man before he even slid into the booth. Without the usual formality of exchanging names, he gave Hamilton a cursory handshake, then immediately got to the point.

'What's your problem?'

The Equalizer's direct approach took Hamilton aback. 'Who are you?'

'Will knowing that make a difference to your trouble?'

Giving it a brief thought, Hamilton shook his head.

'Then tell me what it is,' continued McCall.

Hamilton avoided the Equalizer's clear eyes which both intimidated and distracted him; instead, he looked out of the large plate glass window to the green exterior of the UN, and to the Borough of Queens across the river.

'I'm a groundhog, you know,' he began with a self-deprecating snort. McCall didn't quite catch his meaning. 'That's what my wife calls me. I ferret away at something all day. Keep digging. Rows and rows of figures. Find the flaw. The error. The unexpected.' He paused and finally looked the Equalizer directly in the eye. 'Well, I found it. That's why I was fired.'

'From where?'

'The phone company.'

'What was it you found?'

'Just a number,' answered Hamilton, again gazing nervously about the café, rearranging the silverware in his place setting, taking a sip of water. 'An account, a file, a locked sequence. I don't know. 0900. It doesn't exist. But it's there.

I know it's there. I called a number. Got the Pentagon. But I don't know why.'

McCall listened carefully, committing all the facts to memory. 'What else?'

'Someone tried to run me off the road last night. To kill me. I'm afraid for my family.'

'Who fired you?'

'Jim Olsen.'

'And he's . . .'

'A vice-president in charge of Communications. I worked for him twenty-two years. Don't believe we've said more than "good morning; close out that file, Bill; say hello to Ellen; Merry Christmas" in all that time . . . some communicator, huh?'

While Hamilton was relating the circumstances surrounding his job and firing, the Equalizer weighed the possibilities and the danger. If Hamilton wasn't imagining things, and someone had tried to kill him, then the situation would be very complex and the stakes high. Whoever struck would try again. Hamilton couldn't be too careful.

'Is there somewhere you can go?' McCall asked him. 'Out of the city?'

Hamilton thought for a moment, then answered, 'I've got a cousin in Philly. Haven't seen him in years. He's always saying we've got to get the families together.'

McCall moved in closer, instructing Hamilton very firmly, directly and clearly. 'Tell him you're taking him up on his offer today. Don't use your phone. Call him from a phone booth. I'll pick you up at home at four o'clock. Don't answer your telephone. Don't go out anywhere. If anything happens, call my number. I've got a machine on it and I call in every hour. Do you understand?'

The enormity of the situation diminished Hamilton's capacity for understanding or his ability to think logically. McCall made it sound too easy, too rational.

'What can you do?' Hamilton queried hopelessly. 'This is the phone company! That's like taking on the US Government.'

The Equalizer allowed himself a small smile. 'I'll feel right at home . . .'

His cryptic meaning escaped Hamilton, who had other considerations on his mind. 'How much is this going to cost me?'

The question seemed unimportant to the Equalizer, who dismissed the question – and Hamilton – by rising from the table.

'We'll work that out,' he said cheerfully. 'Let's just not make it your life.'

NINE

The jazz class in the third floor aerobics studio on Broadway ran longer than usual. It had been a tough workout. Colleen knew she would feel better for it later on; for the moment, she felt completely exhausted. The loft room was so warm from all the perspiring spandex-suited bodies that the windows had steamed over. A look at the wall clock told her she didn't have much time to get the shopping done and return home to Sarah.

Having quickly showered and changed, Colleen put on what she called her 'sleeping bag coat' (which looked just like a tufted burgundy sleeping bag), black stretch pants, and high-top black boots. She hoped the coat's insulated hood would keep her head warm and ward off pneumonia. She looked a mess. No big deal. She wasn't addressing a parents and teachers meeting at the school where she taught art, and, God knows, she wasn't going to run into anyone she knew in the market.

Everyone else must have decided to go shopping on the way home from work. The narrow aisles were packed with carts and mothers with strollers. Like a contestant on a game show racing against the clock to fill her cart, Colleen sped down the aisles, pulling items off the shelves as fast as she could move.

At the end of the generic foods section, Colleen was checking out the newest offerings with the black and white labels without trademarks. She always felt she was beating the system if she discovered a new item which would have cost her twice the price under a brand name label. It was one of the few pleasures she had in shopping. While busily studying the shelves, she sensed a presence standing beside her at the end of the aisle. She turned and gasped.

Steve was standing there calm as you please, eating a candy bar with all the menace and sexual suggestion one could put into the act of consuming chocolate. Spinning around, Colleen fled from generic foods into the safety of laundry detergents. Pausing in the aisle, she was relieved to find that Steve hadn't pursued her.

Pitching some soap and window cleaner into the cart, she made a dash for the checkout stand. She prayed the lines wouldn't be congested and she could get out of there without much further ado. She was disappointed. Even the express line was a long wait. Impatient, she took her place in the shortest line she could find.

She was counting her money when she saw someone in the adjacent line signalling her.

Steve. Finishing off the candy bar. Obscenely licking his fingers.

She wanted to scream. She stifled the urge, hoping that if she ignored him he would go away. He wouldn't. Gesturing, he offered her the space in front of him. Colleen gripped the handle of the cart. Her knuckles were white. She couldn't suppress her rage any longer. Her voice seemed detached from her as she started screaming hysterically at him.

'Stay away from me! Don't call me any more! Stay away from my child! I'll kill you! I swear to God I'll stab you through the heart!'

All activity around her came to a sudden halt. The shoppers in the market were used to screaming lunatics on the streets but not in the safe surroundings of the grocery store. An elderly woman standing behind Colleen took her handcart and shuffled off into another line. The check-out girls froze. The grocery tabs would have to wait until they could find the source of the commotion and feel secure that some mad shopper wasn't going to lunge behind their cash registers.

Steve feigned embarrassment, pretending he was a nice guy who was being wrongly chastised by a crazy woman to whom he'd only showed politeness.

'Never seen her before in my life,' he told the startled people around him.

Incensed by his gentleman act, Colleen raised her voice even louder. 'Get out! Get out of my sight!'

'I'm going, lady,' he said, apologetically. 'Just take it easy. You can have my place in line. I'm outta here.' Shrugging his shoulders to impress the onlookers with his boyish innocence, he jumped the railing and beat a hasty retreat through the automatic door.

After Steve fled out of sight, Colleen's fury was long in subsiding. Clutching her cart, she felt her entire body still trembling from raw emotion. When she looked up, the shoppers ahead of her were clearing out of her way to wait for another register. If she could have laughed at the situation, she might have seen the humour in the effect she had on the crowd. She'd never have guessed it was so easy to get to the head of the line.

Blanketed in the heavy snowfall, New Bedford, Connecticut, a small, quaint New England town with a main street, a town square, and a commuter railroad station, resembled a Currier and Ives painting. Farther up the hill from the main part of town was the residential section, home of the William Hamiltons. Unlike many of the old clapboard houses which dated to the Revolutionary War, the Hamilton's house was modern.

51

The Equalizer arranged to meet Bill and Ellen Hamilton to chauffeur them out of the area to the safety of their relatives in Philadelphia, usually a two-hour trip by car. McCall was taking them in his car, a sleek, shiny, black Jaguar which the Agency had purchased for him to his specifications. Having placed the Hamilton's bags in the boot of the car, McCall motioned for them to climb into the back seat. Then the Equalizer took the wheel.

The snowfall whitewashed the landscape like a hazy gauze, making driving and visibility difficult. The Equalizer switched on his headlights to penetrate the murk. Because of the snow and its glare, McCall was oblivious to the black Plymouth parked down the street from the Hamilton's. The Plymouth had tailed the Equalizer from the City. Olsen was driving. Beside him was a distinguished-looking gentleman with receding grey hair. Though Gardner's pin-stripes make him appear to be a fellow phone company executive, the pump gun in his lap which was concealed by a blanket defined his true profession. As Olsen observed the Equalizer's Jaguar pulling away from the Hamilton's kerb, he picked up a walkie-talkie hand radio. 'They're leaving,' he told his cohorts, then pulled away in pursuit.

The Equalizer's Jaguar moved west along the rolling country road, past trees, over creeks, and old weather-beaten barns. In the back seat of the car, the Hamiltons held each others' hands and sorrowfully watched the land-scape slipping by.

They had been travelling nearly fifteen minutes when they approached an intersection. The Plymouth, keeping its distance, had the Jaguar's tail lights within striking distance. Gardner stroked the pump gun. Olsen stared intently ahead. He saw McCall and the Hamiltons pass the intersection. A black Mercedes with Leonard Manetti and two armed, heavy men edged out into the intersection. Manetti and Olsen continued to plot their course of action over the walkie-talkie radios. Olsen accelerated the Plymouth through the intersection; the Mercedes followed suit. While the cars increased speed and began gaining on the Jaguar, the two gruff henchmen in the Mercedes checked the rifles resting on their laps. If Gardner's pump gun didn't get the sitting ducks in the Jag, their rifles would finish the job.

As the visibility grew clearer, the Equalizer drove faster down the two-lane country highway. A forest now flanked the highway on both sides. Hamilton and his wife exchanged glances. This wasn't the usual route to Philadelphia, at least none they'd ever heard of. After twisting around a few more curves – and with no sign of a main highway in sight – Hamilton finally leaned forward into the front seat.

'Where are we going?'

McCall was terse, to the point. 'Small airfield. A private plane's going to take you to Philadelphia. A car will meet you there and drive you to your cousin. All part of the service. No questions asked.'

Hamilton seemed satisfied with his answer, though something else suddenly disturbed him. The Equalizer's eyes instinctively darted to the rear-view mirror and lingered there. He saw the black blur of the Plymouth deliberately closing the distance. Gardner leaned out the window with the pump gun. No sooner had the Equalizer spotted the suspicious car and the tip of the gun than he wrenched the wheel, causing the Jag to swerve drastically to avoid being a target. He screamed a warning at the Hamiltons: 'Get down!'

The violent jerk of the car almost threw the couple onto the floor of the car. Falling into each other, Hamilton and Ellen crouched as closely to the floor as possible.

Gaining ground, the Plymouth raced down the road towards the Jaguar. McCall pressed his foot to the accelerator pedal. But the Plymouth had the momentum and was quickly upon the Jaguar, pulling around alongside McCall.

The pump gun was aimed at the Equalizer. Suddenly, as the hitman pumped the gun barrel, the Jaguar dropped back. McCall's timing was perfect. Gardner's blast blew into the front side window. Shards of flying glass stung the

Equalizer's face; otherwise he was unharmed. Glass scattered across the dashboard. Maintaining his cool reason, the Equalizer anticipated the Plymouth's next move and swung the Jaguar's wheel hard left.

Olsen wasn't prepared for a broadside attack on his car. He lacked the stomach for this deadly game anyway, and the Equalizer had been at it most of his life. Olsen sickened at the crunch of metal as the Jag struck the passenger side. The wheel spun wildly out of control under his fingers. Olsen exchanged a panicked glance at Gardner, whose hands still gripped the pump gun. Despair overcame Olsen as he realized there was no way he could keep the Plymouth on the treacherous country road.

Continuously rammed broadside by McCall's car, the Plymouth hit a patch of ice which helped to send it sailing off the road embankment into a small copse. Across the road, the Jaguar also swerved. McCall fought to regain control as the car plunged off into the trees. Surprised to find he wasn't injured, Olsen regained his composure and drove back onto the road, from which he spied the Equalizer and the Hamiltons barrelling through the densely grouped trees on the right-hand side of the road.

The branches made a nerve-racking grating sound as they scraped across the roof of the Jaguar. The Hamiltons bounced with the rough terrain and held onto each other without any idea what was going on outside. They dared not raise their heads to find out. Meanwhile McCall wasn't stopped by the overgrowth. Despite the branches snatching at the windscreen and obstructing his vision, he ploughed deeper into the wooded area. The trees came up on him so fast that he barely avoided several head-on collisions. A man without *his* combat driving skills would have been dead by now, and the Hamiltons would be in the boot with their baggage.

Avoiding tree trunks and knocking down saplings, McCall ploughed through the forest. Coming from behind, the Plymouth was following his tracks through the heavily wooded area. McCall had hoped to damage the car enough to put it out of commission; he hadn't succeeded. The assassin and his pump gun obviously weren't out of commission either. Gardner leaned out the Plymouth's windows and fired again. The gun blast echoed through the woods. The bullets found their mark in the Jaguar's rear window, slamming into it and shattering the glass into a shower of shards. Terrified, the Hamilton's covered their heads as the glass pellets rained down on them.

'Dammit, what's going on?' Hamilton shrieked.

'Nothing. Just stay down,' the Equalizer ordered.

The couple bounced around again on the floor while the Jaguar crashed through some hedges which opened into a clearing. Out in the open, with room to manoeuvre at last, McCall slewed the car around. McCall reached up to the roof of the car and pulled back a sliding panel, exposing the various parts of a high-powered rifle affixed there. In the brief lull before the Plymouth descended upon them again, he hastily assembled the rifle with machine-line efficiency and precision. Before the Plymouth had exploded out of the foliäge, he jumped out of the car, loading the rifle as he took up his position beside the Jaguar.

He heard the roar of the dark Plymouth's engine before he saw the car burst through the hedge into the clearing; by then, his sights were fixed on the target. He fired twice at the oncoming car. Its front tyres popped in the wake of the gun's explosion and rubber flew out to the sides of the clearing. Olsen screamed. Gardner dropped his pump gun. The landscape hurtled up toward the two men as the car swerved out of control and headed for the frozen river at the clearing's edge. When it reached the river's banks, the car dipped down at an angle, its front end striking the ice and sending the car into a flip. When the car landed on the roof with a metal-crunching thud, the ice cracked into a groaning fracture.

Emotionally shaken but unharmed, Olsen and Gardner scrambled out of the car windows. As they struggled to get their footing, they slipped on the ice, which was fast breaking up from the impact of the car on its surface. The sound of the fissures widening made for an eerie, ominous noise in the silent woods. Off in the distance, they heard the sound of the approaching Mercedes, Manetti and his reserve troops having hung back until now.

The Plymouth began to sink through the hole it had punched in the ice. While the fissures travelled at a faster pace, Olsen and Gardner gained their footing and raced against nature. Scurrying across the ice toward the embankment, they looked on in dismay at the sight of the Equalizer poised for a frontal attack on the approaching Mercedes.

When Manetti and his two men emerged from the thicket, they were met with two gun blasts from the Equalizer's rifles. Their windscreen looked something like the river ice breaking up. Uninjured by the gun blast itself, Manetti couldn't see anything through the suddenly crystallized glass; in order to see, he punched a hole in the windscreen. The first thing he saw was a tree racing up to greet them head-on. With lightning reflexes and a quick-swing to the right on the wheel, he managed to skirt the tree. But he was too late to avoid the steep incline. The Mercedes went over it like a skier taking a jump. He and his men survived the jarring landing at the bottom of the ravine. Clambering out of the Mercedes, a frantic Manetti yelled to his cohorts on the ice, 'Get us out of here.'

Certain that his pursuers wouldn't be going anywhere for a while, the Equalizer slid back into the driver's seat and gunned the Jaguar. It sailed smoothly between the hedges and through the forest. There was no more gunfire.

Hamilton peeked his head over the top of the front seat. 'Can we come up now?' he asked meekly.

TEN

The 83rd Precinct of the New York Police Department had seen better days. Erected in the early part of the century, the building had fallen on hard times and municipal budget cuts. It hadn't seen a paint job in years, as attested to by the peeling paint and spray grafitti. The steps leading up to the entrance had been eroded by too many winters of expanding and contracting. By some miracle, the two large lamp globes on either side of the steps had escaped grafitti and destruction by the vandalism rampant in the neighbourhood. There was only a small parking lot to the side of the building; so most of the cars were triple parked – one on the sidewalk, and two in the street. If you drove down the street on a busy day, chances are you'd have to wait for a cop to move one of the blue-and-white cherrytops so you could get through. The neighbours never complained. They had the safest block around.

Inside the precinct house, office space was as much at a premium as parking space outside. Several clerks shared an office, and sometimes more than one occupied the same desk. Sitting out in the halls along with the wooden benches for the public were temporary desks for cops and personnel. On the main floor of the precinct station, weary detectives sat at rows of desks. The phones rang constantly. Teletypes clacked along the walls. Typewriters provided a staccato beat to the other officer noises. Besides a phone on every desk there was one common fixture: a bottle of aspirin.

Through this cramped, under-staffed precinct trooped the regular hookers, drunks, and drug dealers from the street. Most of them were familiar to the cops of the 83rd; some were on a bantering first-name basis. New York was a small town at heart, especially where criminals were concerned.

The Equalizer didn't rate as a criminal, but he had more than a passing familiarity with cops about town. One of them, Lieutenant Burnett – a brittle, highly-strung, bright cop in his late forties – met McCall in the foyer and escorted him through the main bureau to the rear of the precinct.

Like McCall, Burnett was not a man to mince words. 'Any reason why I should help you, McCall? Think hard.'

'Some shared cups of coffee,' the Equalizer responded, thinking that as good a reason as any.

The lieutenant spared McCall a reaction; instead, he ushered him into a cubicle of an office, separated from the masses by a grimy glass partition with his name stencilled on the door. The clouded glass was all that separated Burnett from his rank-and-file fellow officers on the other side. The noise got through anyway. McCall quickly surveyed the messy office. The desk was cluttered with half-empty coffee cups which sat on top of papers which may well have been collecting cobwebs by now. Despite the sloppy appearance, Burnett could lay his finger on a file in an instant.

Burnett sat back in his swivel chair and gave McCall a wry grin. 'So you're a security officer now. Respectable.'

'I wouldn't go that far.'

Burnett reached for a lukewarm cup of coffee and

sipped. 'How many employees in this security company of yours?' 'One,' McCall replied, the irony not escaping Burnett. 'Good men are hard to find.'

Burnett reached under a coffee cup, then under a pile of files under the cup, and finally pulled out a newspaper, which he flashed at McCall.

'The "Equalizer." Cute ad. Till someone blows your head off. You've got no backup in these streets.'

'I work alone. You know that.' To remind him, McCall reiterated his request. 'Licence XTJ 295. Black Mercedes, '84 plates.'

Burnett had obliged the request. Picking up another piece of paper, he handed it to the Equalizer.

'Leonard Manetti. A senior vice-president in the phone company.' The Equalizer wasn't surprised by the phone company connection, though the senior level of the employees struck him as unusual. 'What's your problem?' asked Burnett, 'Your bill too high? You gonna wreck the place?'

McCall rose to go. 'I'll try and restrain myself. Thanks, Jeff,' he said, opening the door.

Burnett got up and came around his desk. 'McCall . . .'

The Equalizer turned around and faced the lieutenant. 'Yes?'

'Crime is organized. You're not. This isn't 'Nam . . . or Africa . . . or Central America. This is the Big Apple, and you don't know what real guerrilla warfare is like until you hit those streets.'

McCall was gratified by his concern. 'I'll keep that in mind,' he said softly, and closed the door behind him.

Shaking his head, Burnett slumped back into his chair and thought about McCall. The guy was decent. And smart. Too bad he wasn't smart enough to heed his warning and save his hide.

McCall glided through the desks outside Burnett's office. Even though the evening was just getting started, the precinct already had its hands full, or so it appeared to him. The waiting lobby near the front entrance was a gallery of drawn, anxious faces. As the Equalizer went through the door leading outside, he passed an exhausted officer taking another account from another hysterical woman.

The woman was Colleen Randall. In the aftermath of the encounter with the menacing Steve at the supermarket, she was still venting her fury. Her face became florid from her frustration. Wouldn't anyone listen to her? Officer Goldman was going through the motions, but he wasn't as sympathetic or assuring as she had expected a New York cop to be.

'Mrs Randall,' Goldman explained, straining to be patient, 'the man hasn't come within thirty feet of you. He hasn't even threatened to rape you.'

'It's in his voice,' she cut him off angrily. 'It's what he *doesn't* say; it's what he's implying. Can't you understand that?'

Goldman shook his head. 'There's nothing we can do until . . .'

'Until I get raped,' she lashed out at him, jumping to her feet from the chair beside the desk. 'And then, if I don't wash the evidence away, if I'm not too scared to talk . . . What happens then?' Goldman, intimidated by her outburst, looked at her blankly. 'He gets off.' Although Goldman didn't disagree with her, as a New York City police officer he couldn't admit that she was probably right. 'You've got to stop him before he can hurt me,' she said, changing her tone as she took his arm pleadingly. 'Haul him in. Scare the hell out of him.'

Goldman had heard this story too many times before. How could he explain to this lady that he felt every bit as frustrated as she?

'That's police harassment, Mrs Randall,' he explained, going by the book. 'We can't even check if he's got a record without a last name. If you could find out . . .'

'Sure,' she shot back, angry again, letting go of his arm. 'I'll make a point to ask him while he's telling me what he's going to do to my body. I have a child, you know. He's scaring her.'

60

'If he's threatened your child,' Officer Goldman explained patiently, 'we can pull him in. But we can't hold him unless . . .'

Again, Colleen cut him off. 'Unless he touches her. He doesn't want my child. Don't you understand? He wants *me*.'

'Change your phone number,' the officer suggested reasonably, even though he knew it would do little to calm her nerves or make her feel more secure. 'Buy new locks.'

'And live locked in my apartment like a frightened animal?' she scoffed. 'Thank you for your time, Lieutenant. I'm sorry I wasted it.'

Before Colleen was even out of the door, Goldman's attention was off of her and on the suspect two cops were dragging inside the precinct house for questioning. Goldman routinely flipped his notebook to the next page and prepared to take down the details.

ELEVEN

The party in the phone company's mid-town headquarters was a celebration to unveil the architectural model of a new modern monolith to be erected for the corporation at a downtown site once considered a haven for derelicts. Thanks to the decision of the phone company and other mega-corporations, the area had now become prime real estate, and the poor were forced to move on and find new homes. But no one at this party would much care what became of the dispossessed. The party-goers had elegant co-ops to go home to; they salved their consciences with the notion that what was best for the phone company was best for America.

The perfume and cigar smoke, in nearly equal proportions, were thick in the corporate boardroom where the festivities were under way. Women in long sequinned gowns flitted from one *hors d'oeuvre* tray to the next. Their husbands, the company executives, clustered in small groups to pat themselves on the back for the new building, make grandiose predictions for the future of themselves and the company, and boast of their own power, all the while wondering if their cummerbunds were too high or their bow ties cockeyed. Their intense conversations were occasionally interrupted by a waiter circulating with champagne. Among the distinguished phone company blue bloods, Manetti, Olsen, and 'security chief' Gardner conspired near an exhibit of phone company installations throughout the country. Though their bodies and egos may have been bruised by their recent mishap with the Equalizer, they appeared none the worse for wear.

The cause of their trouble, McCall, had waltzed into the party without any objections. With his natural air of social assuredness, and the way a tuxedo seemed part of his everyday attire, no one was about to stop the most elegant gentleman at the party from attending. He circulated freely through the room, coolly appraising the loud crowd. Only when the Equalizer began eyeing the door at the end of the board room did the bouncer, Peebles, take notice. As McCall opened the door, Peebles laid a hand on his arm to stop him.

'Where do you work, fella?' Peebles demanded.

'Communications,' McCall answered confidently.

'I don't know you.'

McCall smiled. 'Friend of Bill Hamilton's.'

'He's not with us any longer.'

'Yes, he is,' McCall chided. 'In spirit.' Brushing Peebles aside, he moved through the door and closed it behind him.

The bored, uniformed guard sitting watch before a bank of TV screens in the reception area failed to spot the Equalizer enter the rear of the security station adjacent to the boardroom. The guard studied the monitors, which flashed on different areas of the building from moment to moment. Meanwhile, following instructions Hamilton had given him, the Equalizer moved down a corridor and tried a door marked *STAIRS*. Slipping quietly through the door, he walked down another hallway until he reached a locked door, Hamilton's former office. Taking a small ring of master keys from his pocket, he tried one. Nothing. Then another. The same result. He was in luck with the third try as the key turned the lock. The Equalizer pushed the door open and entered Manetti's office.

On finding himself in the shadowy office, McCall became instantly aware of the swivelling video camera which was suspended from the ceiling in a corner of the room. Hamilton had told him how the system of camera surveillance worked and had drawn him a diagram. McCall moved under the video camera and removed a small, flat Polaroid camera from his coat pocket. Then he pulled over a chair, stood on it, and snapped a photo from the video camera's point of view. When the picture had developed, he attached it in front of the camera lens, focusing the video camera lens accordingly so that the photograph would show up as an empty office on the monitor; that accomplished, he was at liberty to prowl about. The trick worked. A moment later, when the office appeared in sequence on the guard's monitor, it read as deserted.

McCall found Hamilton's computer still intact on his desk, just where Hamilton said it would be. After switching the computer on, he unfolded the piece of paper with Hamilton's written sequence of numbers. A second passed before the series of numbers began appearing on the computer screen. The numbers rotated until at last one number recurred regularly: 0900. He gave the computer the order *DISPLAY 0900*. It responded with *SYNTAX ERROR*. At this juncture, the Equalizer took another look at Hamilton's notes, reading them in the green glow of the computer monitor. Having consulted his instructions, he punched more keys on the computer board. Another pause, this one longer. Then more rotating numbers, followed by symbols. Suddenly the screen went blank. The Equalizer began to wonder what had gone wrong when a series of jumbled letters appeared. He smiled. At last he had what he'd come for.

Reaching over to the dot matrix printer beside the desk, he hit the *ON* button and rolled a sheet of paper through the platen. He hit the print button. The printer whirred quietly, transferring the numbers from the screen onto the paper in a matter of seconds.

While the Equalizer tapped into the phone company's computer files, Colleen Randall was calming her frayed nerves with a hot shower at home. The front door opened and closed. Sarah was probably going down the hall to visit her friends. Colleen wished she'd asked for permission; she'd have to scold her when she returned. Massaging shampoo into her hair, Colleen shouted a loud 'hello' from under the shower head. Sarah didn't answer. Maybe the sound of the water drowned out her voice so Colleen couldn't hear. On the other side of the white plastic shower curtain, Colleen could barely make out the ephemeral shadow of a figure appearing, then disappearing.

'Sarah, is that you, hon? What do you want?'

This time when there was no response, Colleen grew concerned. She quickly turned off the taps, stopping the torrent of water. Pushing her hair back, she squeezed out the water and stood very still in the shower – listening. Silence, save for the noise of the water dripping.

The shadow figure appeared again. Suddenly Colleen's body became tense with dread. She dared not move. Again, the figure vanished. Tentatively, she reached her hand out of the shower and pulled the curtain aside. The bathroom was deserted. She was haunted by the lingering feeling that an ominous presence remained in the house. Stepping out of the tub, she reached for a towel and stepped onto the bath mat. She looked around the bathroom. Everything looked the same. Until she checked the mirror over the sink.

She froze at the appalling sight of the giant letters smeared across the mirror with her lipstick:

YOU CAN'T KEEP ME OUT, COLLEEN. I'LL BE BACK, BABY.

Unconsciously, she bit her knuckles. Her lip trembled. 'He's been in here,' she said to herself, then screamed at the top of her voice, 'Sarah!'

Colleen ran into the living room. The lights were still on, but there was no sign of Sarah. Heading for the kitchen, Colleen grew frantic, her voice breaking. 'Sarah . . .'

Suddenly Sarah came into the living room, dragging her giant Road Runner doll, at least a foot bigger than she, from her small bedroom where she'd been playing by herself. She wondered why her mother, still soaking wet from her shower, was standing in the living room.

'What is it, Mummy?' she asked. Colleen was too shocked and afraid to answer. 'Mummy, you're dripping on the carpet. You always tell me off.'

Without a word, Colleen turned and moved quickly out of the living room to the front door. The three locks, all of them added as per Lieutenant Goldman's suggestion, were now unlocked. Frantically, Colleen re-locked them, though they were obviously a futile defence against her tormentor.

She didn't waste a moment in getting from the door to the makeshift desk in the living room. Taking the day-old newspaper from under a stack of papers, she rifled through the pages.

Her daughter looked at her with a puzzled expression. 'What are you doing?'

'Getting help.'

'For what?'

'For us,' Colleen said, finally spreading out the paper to the ad that had caught her eye. She pulled the phone over and called the Equalizer.

The Equalizer's phone rang at home. But he wasn't there to answer. His phone machine took Colleen's frightened message.

Still in Hamilton's office in the phone company building, McCall grabbed the sheet of paper as the printer automatically rolled out the fan-fold paper. He tore off the sheets containing the number sequences and laid them on the desk. He switched off the printer and the computer. Suddenly he sensed a presence outside the door, the shadow of feet underneath the door crack. A key was turning in the lock.

The Equalizer flew into action, jumping up on the chair and ripping the Polaroid snapshot off the video camera. Before the door opened, he managed to jump down off the chair and stuff the computer printout into a Manilla file. He was ready as a startled guard walked through the door. McCall greeted him with a congenial non-threatening smile.

'Celebration or not,' McCall told him, 'when Mr Manetti needs a file, he gets it. Lock the door after me, will you?'

Innocently enough, McCall passed the guard, who bought McCall's story without question.

McCall pitched the manilla folder in a hallway trash can and hid the papers inside his tuxedo jacket. By the time he reached the lobby again, the boardroom door was opening. Manetti stepped out. Peebles, who had informed Manetti about the suspicious party guest, was behind him, pointing out McCall to him. The Equalizer ignored both of them as he crossed the lobby reception area. But eventually Manetti and Peebles caught up with him.

Manetti stopped him with, 'Thought I knew all of my employees, Mr . . .'

'McCall,' said the Equalizer. 'I'm with the catering service. Everything all right.'

Manetti studied the Equalizer's face. 'Just fine. We've met before.'

'I don't think so.'

'I saw you . . .' Manetti said as he placed the Equalizer's face. 'Today.' He paused, giving the Equalizer a chance to react. He didn't. 'You have excellent taste in automobiles. That's a good-looking Jaguar.'

'Had to put it in for service,' McCall explained wryly. 'Bad road conditions.'

'Bill Hamilton isn't worth it.'

The Equalizer smiled cheerfully. 'He is to me.'

As far as McCall was concerned, the conversation was terminated. He walked away from Manetti.

Mannetti started after him, then thought better of it. There would be plenty of time to take care of this McCall problem after the festivities.

TWELVE

Though he had what he needed from the phone company computer files, his day wasn't over yet. He rang into his answering machine, picked up the message from Colleen, and directed her to the New York Café Restaurant.

More alive at night than it was during the day, the restaurant overflowed with diners. For purely aesthetic reasons, the Equalizer preferred Perry's place in the evening. There were few New York views as breathtaking as the floodlit United Nations Building and the lights across the river in Queens. As he stepped through the entrance, McCall caught Carol's eye. Mixing drinks at the bar, she gave him the high-sign and motioned for him to come over. Perry noticed him too and greeted him at the bar.

'Twice in one day. We're honoured.'

McCall laughed. 'Sing something from *Top Banana*.'

Top Banana was the one show that had made John Perry famous for a moment in Broadway musical theatre history. McCall knew his old friend never missed a chance to sing his favourite number.

Perry sang, '"You're so beautiful that, that Lana turned green, Liz, Ava, Greer and Arlene, run second to you."' The Equalizer and Carol applauded. 'You're the only person who remembers my New York career.'

McCall grinned. 'Now we're both on Broadway.'

'I wouldn't be here if it wasn't for you,' Perry told him gratefully.

'Try and forget that.'

'You don't forget the man who saved your life. You just forget the pain. That's why I bought this place. It's full of life and energy and show-business talk. No codes to be broken. No sniper to fire at you. No need to be rescued by the Equalizer. Just good-natured verbal assassination.'

'Sounds violent to me,' laughed McCall.

'Worse if you're a theatre critic.' Perry nodded towards the rear of the restaurant. 'A young lady's waiting for you at the last booth. She's pretty shaken up.'

The Equalizer recognized Colleen as a client by her nervous disposition. Like Hamilton before her, Colleen had been driven to the point where she was twisting her hands together in frustration. The thought of Hamilton crossed his mind. McCall imagined that Hamilton and Ellen would be safely ensconced at his cousin's in Philly by now. That would give McCall the time needed to help this woman.

'What's your problem,' he asked Colleen gently as he slipped into the booth opposite her.

'Is that how you say hello?'

'My clients don't usually have time for amenities,' he explained.

'Who are your clients?'

'People like you.'

He noticed her hand trembling on the table. He reached out and took it, and she squeezed his tightly.

'I'm just so scared,' she told him, tears brimming up in her eyes.

'Of whom?'

'He says his name is Steve. I think he first saw me in the supermarket. He's been hounding me for a month. Phone

69

calls, casual meetings, sexual innuendo. I thought I could handle it. But tonight he was in my apartment.'

Clearing his throat, McCall asked quietly, 'Did he . . .'

'No, no,' she replied, shaking her head. 'It's all part of his game plan: suggest, insinuate, needle, make me wait for my rape. I'd move, But where can I go? I can't afford to do that. My rent's controlled. My daughter's so happy in school. She has her friends.' For a moment, Colleen's voice grew stronger, defiant. 'Anyway, why the hell should I go anywhere? It's my life and he's destroying it.'

Her wall of defiance collapsed and she dissolved in tears. Angry with herself for crying, she took the cloth napkin and dabbed at her face, smearing her mascara. Emotionally drained, she stared out at the East River while listening to McCall's gently prodding questions.

'Did you go to the police?'

She nodded. 'They're up to their eyes in murders and gang warfare and don't need to hear from a hysterical divorcee who *might* be raped by a guy who hasn't even threatened it yet.'

'What *have* you done?'

'I put in new locks – three of them – but he still got in. I've gone through my list of friends who could spend the night. They can't hold my hand forever.' She looked at McCall, who regarded her emphatically. 'I just can't stand it any longer. Your ad said if the odds were against me . . . well, they are. What can you do?'

'Equalize the odds,' McCall answered directly. 'Put them in your favour.'

The concept of putting the odds in her favour was beyond her grasp at the moment. 'How do I do that?'

'I have ways.' His simple assurance made her feel better. She trusted him. She was willing to co-operate. 'What does Steve look like?'

Opening her purse, Colleen pulled out a pastel drawing of her tormentor. The likeness captured him perfectly, right down to his psychotic, candy-chewing grin.

'I'm an art teacher,' Colleen explained, handing McCall

the sketch. 'I did this from memory, but its pretty accurate. I don't know who he is or where he lives.'

'You don't have to find him,' McCall smiled assuredly. 'That's my job.'

'He's been hanging around my apartment building every day at four in the afternoon. That's when I usually get home from shopping.'

As McCall leaned closer to her and gave her firm, specific instructions, Colleen listened attentively. 'I want you to call me every hour, from six in the morning until you go to sleep. I have a machine on my phone. I call in every hour.'

'If I see him?'

'You call. If it's across a crowded street, you call. I'll be there. He won't bother you after that.'

It sounded too good to be true. Colleen prayed he was right. His sensitivity, caring, and directness touched her deeply. She didn't know how she could ever thank him. McCall read the sudden worry in her face.

'I don't have a lot of money to pay you,' she told him apologetically, 'but I can sell some bonds and . . .'

Interrupting politely, McCall said, 'We'll work that out later.'

'I'm just so scared,' she said, looking away from him and across the restaurant.

Again, the Equalizer reached across and gave her hand a reassuring squeeze.

'You're going to be all right. I'll take care of you. No one's going to hurt you, Colleen. Now, let me take you home.'

They drove uptown along the FDR drive in the Equalizer's Jag and cut across town at 79th Street. McCall sped from the East Side to the West Side, travelling Central Park and listened to a more detailed account of Colleen's terrifying experiences with her pursuer.

After he deposited Colleen at her apartment on West 81st Street, he stayed with her until they made certain she was safe for the evening.

'I sent my little girl to a friend's place,' she told him as she showed him out. 'Just for a few days.'

71

'Good idea.'

'I feel I should know the name of the man who's giving me peace of mind.'

The Equalizer deliberated whether to tell her, and decided no harm would be done. 'Robert McCall.'

'Thank you, Mr McCall.'

'I'll be close,' he informed her, 'even if you can't see me.'

'That does make me feel better. Good night.'

She closed the door. McCall walked out of the building. That night, Colleen slept fitfully, but better than she had in weeks.

THIRTEEN

The Equalizer didn't make a habit of playing racquetball with Agency operatives. But he needed a favour, and Brahms was the best man to handle it. Under the bright lights and white glare of the New York health club's court, McCall and Brahms took turns slamming the ball against the wall. Never one to be in great physical shape, the overweight Brahms played racquetball because he thought he should, not because he enjoyed it. The Equalizer was quickly driving him into the ground. Finally Brahms couldn't take it anymore. His legs ached. He was out of breath. And he looked like he'd been swimming. By contrast, the Equalizer gracefully glided across the court, not stopping until he saw Brahms throw down his racket.

'I'm sweating like a pig,' Brahms complained to him. 'You look like you just stepped off the cover of *GQ*. I shouldn't even be talking to you. It could be bad for my health.'

'How is your health, Brahms?' the Equalizer asked, handing him a clean towel to dry himself off.

'Blood pressure high, cholesterol high, self-esteem low. So what else is new?' McCall laughed sympathetically. 'Your resignation. That was new; that was exciting. I don't know anyone who's ever done that and walked away.'

The Equalizer was suddenly all business. 'I need a favour.'

Brahms gazed at McCall as if he was crazy. 'You want me put up against a wall and shot? I had to check my glasses to make sure they weren't bugged.'

'I know I'm putting you at risk.'

Brahms finished towelling off his face and looked at the Equalizer, fondly remembering. 'I seem to recall a time I put *you* at risk. You gonna be okay?'

'What do you think?'

'You're a code red, in case you weren't aware – a top security violation. Control's hands are tied.'

'I dealt with that,' he said, referring to the would-be assassin at Rockefella Plaza. 'But speaking of codes, I need one broken.'

Brahms shook his head. 'Same old McCall, only hears the music he wants to hear.'

'You like to hear Brahms,' McCall teased him.

'As a matter of fact, I listened to Brahms' *Number 4, E Minor Opus 98* last night. It was wonderful, as usual.' Becoming serious, Brahms asked, 'What kind of code?'

The Equalizer reached into his gym bag and pulled out the computer print-outs.

'It's a series of something.'

'Very helpful,' Brahms said facetiously.

'The key to it is 0900.'

'My favourite number,' he continued with the same flippant attitude. 'When do you want this?'

The Equalizer gave Brahms an ingratiating smile. 'Tonight.' Glancing at his watch, McCall noticed it was time to check in on Colleen. She would be getting home from the market about now.

McCall's rented Ford sedan got him to Colleen's Upper West Side Neighbourhod by 3.55, five minutes before the time she usually arrived at her apartment. Although his Jag had only been in the shop since morning, McCall missed it and felt out of place in the rented vehicle. Slowly, he cruised down Colleen's tree-lined block. He spotted her coming towards him from the opposite direction. She seemed more easy-going than she had last night. Her face was more relaxed, happier, younger looking.

Keeping some distance from her building, McCall observed her as she neared the stoop of her building and paused to fish the keys from her purse. In the moment she searched for her keys, Steve, spying on her from the doorway next door, stepped out onto the street and took her by surprise, humming softly as he came up behind her.

'Colleen,' he sang mockingly. 'Hey, baby. Talk to me.'

Moving quickly towards her building, she looked straight ahead, refusing to acknowledge his presence or make eye contact with him. Fumbling, she got the key-ring out of her purse. The panic began to well up inside of her. Please, God, if she could only find the right key.

'Right here . . .' he mocked her. 'I'm behind you . . . your guardian angel . . . waiting for you . . .'

Her hand shook as she tried desperately to get the key. She thought about running into the foyer, then realized she would be better off running down the street. At least someone might see her there. Once he had her behind the door, there was no telling what could happen. It never occurred to her to scream. All she could think of was the key.

Meanwhile, from a short distance down the street, the Equalizer quickly sized up the situation. Using the sketch Colleen had drawn, he recognized the man stalking her as Steve. He gunned the car's engine, raced down the street, and, bearing down on Steve, jumped the sidewalk with the sedan. Metal trash cans went flying with a deafening racket. Colleen finally screamed.

Dodging the car, the nimble-footed Steve leaped to one side of it. The Equalizer's intrusion gave Colleen the time she needed to get her key and bolt into the safety of her apartment building. Reversing the car, McCall prepared for another assault on Steve. But before the car could lunge in his direction again, Steve attempted to get away. The Equalizer had out-manoeuvred him, this time using the sedan to force Steve into an alleyway.

Steve imagined he'd be safe once he got into the alley. He'd escape through the back, or climb up a fire escape if he had to; but he was out of luck. There were no fire escapes and no outlets. The alley was a cul-de-sac. Cornered, Steve ran towards the back of the alley as the rapidly approaching car threatened to squeeze him against its rear brick wall. Gasping for breath, he ran in hopes of jumping over the top of the wall. To his dismay, he saw it was rimmed with barbed wire.

The oncoming car was only a few feet behind him now. Steve could hear its deadly engine virtually on top of him. His back against the wall, he whirled around in desperation. His eyes flashed a plea of mercy at the Equalizer.

Just as the car was about to pin him to the wall, it stopped. Steve felt as though the wind had been knocked out of him. Leaning over, he caught his breath, looking up only when he heard the car door open and the Equalizer step out. A rush of adrenalin propelled Steve forward in an attempt to run past the Equalizer. But McCall reached out and grabbed him, throwing him back against the brick wall. Still gasping for breath, and scared that he would die at the hands of this hit man, Steve stared at the Equalizer with wild eyes.

McCall pulled a .38 automatic out of his pocket. Steve was certain he was doomed.

'Don't kill me!' he pleaded. 'I haven't got any money! Take what I've got! Take it all.'

His hand against the young man's throat, the Equalizer increased the pressure and brought up the gun to his head.

'Colleen Randall,' McCall said slowly and deliberately. 'You've had your fun at her expense. You're not going to call her, or see her, or go to her daughter's school, or get anywhere near her ever again. Because if I hear you've been walking down the same street she's on, I'm going to kill you.'

White with fear, Steve nodded his head in understanding, and after a moment – long enough to let the message sink in – the Equalizer let him go. As soon as he felt McCall release his grip, Steve bolted past the sedan and into the street. McCall looked up to see more snow flurries beginning. He put the gun back in his pocket and went to Colleen's apartment to check on her.

Even after the Equalizer told her what happened on the street, she continued to look out the window, down to the phone booth on the street. She still expected to see Steve lurking there. But there was no sign of him.

'You won't hear from him again,' McCall assured her. 'Guys like that are frightened. It's all talk. No action. He won't be back.'

Colleen contemplated out loud, saying, 'He'll just find some other poor girl to terrify.'

'That's not your problem,' McCall told her bluntly. 'Or mine.' She nodded in agreement. 'At least for right now. But just in case, keep your daughter where she is. Go about your daily routine. Call my number and leave a message on my machine every hour up to midnight for the rest of the week.'

McCall noticed she remained ill at ease and continued to be preoccupied with looking at the street. 'If I *do* see him?'

'Call me right away.'

In the wake of this still fresh ordeal, all Colleen could do was shut her eyes to block out the awful prospect of having to endure the likes of it – or worse – again.

FOURTEEN

'Dogs eat better than I do,' complained Brahms.

In McCall's living room that evening, Brahms humoured his former comrade, who had just placed a large plate of cooked beef in front of his Irish setter. The dog happily devoured it, never minding that his master had invited company over to his apartment for cocktails. After tending to his dog, the Equalizer mixed and served his guest a drink.

'Mildred doesn't trust any food that's not frozen,' Brahms laughed, straining to keep the conversation light. 'Her mother was engaged to a Bird's Eye salesman.'

The joke wasn't lost entirely on McCall, who smiled wanly. Taking a seat in the chair opposite Brahms, he sipped on his Scotch and water.

'What have you got?' he asked Brahms point blank.

Brahms handed him back the computer sheet the Equalizer had given him at the racketball court earlier in the day.

'Phone numbers.' He forced another grin. 'What else do you expect from the telephone directory? It's quite a little black book. There's one of particular interest – the top one is a phone number in the Pentagon no one is supposed to have without a five-star clearance. Next one's in the Oval Office. The next one belongs to Senator Jim Blaine. And I don't think the phone company's backing his Presidential campaign.'

Well aware of Blaine's trust-busting, anti-corporate reputation as a US senator, McCall weighed the possibility of his opponents using Watergate-style dirty tricks to ruin Blaine's reputation or smear him politically.

'Bugged phones,' McCall suggested.

Brahms raised an eyebrow. 'Who could do it better? It has to be someone high up, using the equipment without the other directors knowing. What we in the Agency would call a renegade cell.' McCall nodded his agreement with Brahms' assessment. Brahms continued: 'Some important people's phone calls could be embarrassing if played back to an eager public.'

'Particularly a man in Senator Blaine's vulnerable position.'

'Yeah,' Brahms said, growing uncomfortable with the ramifications of the hot information he'd acquired on the sly for his ex-comrade-in-arms. 'I caught your ad,' he said, cheerfully changing the subject to a topic less awkward for him. 'I thought I was the only one who ever called you the "Equalizer".'

'There are others.'

'Yeah, *now*. But I made it up.'

McCall raised his glass to Brahms, giving credit where credit was due. The two men clinked glasses in a silent toast.

Brahms felt himself becoming suddenly sentimental, a dangerous emotion for an intelligence operative to indulge. 'At the risk of sounding like someone who cares – will you retire? Go to the country! Mend fences! Take long walks! Get the hell out of the firing line.'

'Too late,' McCall replied, shrugging off Brahms' well-intentioned advice.

'It's in your blood, huh? That's too bad. I thought maybe you were one of the smart ones.'

While Brahms rambled on, the Equalizer donned his glasses and leafed through the computer pages, going down the phone numbers Brahms had transcribed from the coded letters in the phone company's secret computer files.

'Thanks for this, Brahms.'

Brahms sloughed it off with his usual irreverent insouciance. 'It only took me six hours. Don't get me wrong. I can afford the time. But you haven't got much of it left.' Leaning forward, he raised his voice and delivered a passionate, heart-felt warning intended to shake up McCall. At the very least the dramatic tactic got the Equalizer's attention. 'Will you listen to me for once in your life, Robert? Get out of New York and go somewhere no one is scared of you.'

McCall considered Brahms' sincerity for a moment, then calmly looked at him, saying, 'Good-bye, Brahms.'

Frustrated, Brahms sighed, defeated by his sense of futility. 'Sure,' he said, and rose to his feet. 'I'll cry at your funeral.' Overcome, he looked at McCall for what he thought would be the last time. 'So long, my friend,' he said, and saw himself out into the hallway.

McCall heard the door close behind Brahms. He continued to weigh the evidence in his hands. There wasn't much he could do with the Pentagon or White House phone numbers, but Senator James Blaine had a New York office on the East Side, not far from the Equalizer's apartment. Coincidentally, McCall had seen on the news that Blaine would be holding a rally there this evening. If he left immediately, the Equalizer thought, he could get there just as the senator was addressing his loyal campaign workers.

The TV crews and their trucks were already parked outside Blaine headquarters when the Equalizer arrived. It was a clear, crisp November night. Leaning into the wind, McCall felt the chilling air penetrate his long, olive green camel-hair coat. He turned his collar up to the cold and damp. Through the large storefront window of the campaign offices, McCall observed a jubilant crowd geared up for a party. The scene looked warm and inviting.

Security was lax at the entrance to the headquarters. Anyone could have walked in off the street. The Equalizer did. Smiling at a campaign worker, he asked for a Jim Blaine button, which she gladly pinned to his coat for him. Now the Equalizer would look right at home.

Blaine's face was plastered over every square inch of the vast, featureless room. He looked out from badges, posters, placards, giant photographs, number stickers, and pamphlets. In various corners of the room, you could even take your pick of selected Jim Blaine videos, depicting the candidate's many images: family man, regular guy, statesman, political strategist.

The candidate himself was a Kennedyesque politician who carried himself with the assured bearing of a senator. Older than John Kennedy when he ran for President, Jim Blaine nonetheless had his youthful, twinkling, lively eyes and an engaging public smile. His full head of tousled hair, which might have made him too youthful looking, was tinged with just enough grey to convince voters of his maturity.

As McCall moved towards the raised platform at the front of the room, he spotted Jim Blaine delivering a speech from the podium. Blaine was flanked by local politicians supporting his candidacy, as well as by his young campaign staff. The lights of TV camera crews flooded the stage while Blaine wrapped up his speech to the enthusiastic audience.

'When we're in Washington, I'm going to honour that faith as I honour my family, my heritage, and my country.' A roar went up from the crowd. Blaine, buoyed by the support, stepped back from the microphone and paused for dramatic effect. 'We're going to the White House!'

McCall had to hand it to the guy; he had good timing and was a master at working a crowd. Blaine's declaration set off a loud cheer in the hall. The candidate smiled broadly, waving his hands over his head. Flashbulbs exploded as news photographers snapped pictures of Blaine stepping down from the podium. Following behind his campaign managers who forged a path through the cheering crowd, Blaine continued to shake hands with supporters and local officials.

Politely but firmly, the Equalizer squeezed through the packed house towards the raised platform where he intercepted the security men surrounding the senator. McCall stepped forward and flashed an apparently authentic 'government' identification card which designated him an Agency official.

'Official business,' McCall shouted over the din of the throng. 'Clear a path, boys. Government business.'

The security men trusted the authority in McCall's demeanour, which was corroborated by the identification card. Face to face with the senator, the Equalizer was blocked access by a harried, young, balding frenetic campaign manager who was worried about the senator making his next appointment on time. He tried ignoring the Equalizer's card. Finally the senator himself, wondering what the commotion was all about, intervened.

'Senator Blaine,' said McCall, 'I need to talk to you about an important matter.'

The exasperated manager stepped in argumentatively. 'Look, can't this wait? The senator's very tired and I've told you people . . .'

McCall cut him off and addressed Blaine directly. 'This is about blackmail.'

The Senator's public smile vanished, and he allowed McCall to accompany him through a side door into his awaiting limousine which whisked them away to Blaine's Fifth Avenue apartment.

The apartment had been in the Blaine family for two generations, a large, elegant home designed in the style of the French Beaux Arts period. The walls were of heavy plaster with inset marble columns to match the floors. The high ceilings and massive ironwork windows overlooking Central Park gave the apartment the look of a palace. A massive vaulted skylight in the living room transformed the room with its many tropical plants into a conservatory.

The apartment's rich furnishings and magnificent architecture didn't go unnoticed by the Equalizer. But he had little time to dwell on the senator's taste in antiques. Declining a drink, McCall immediately asked to see the senator's study from where he did much of his business when in the city. Blaine ushered him into the room, which put the Equalizer in mind of the opulence of the JP Morgan Library. Overlooking the leather- and gold-bound volumes in the floor-to-ceiling bookshelves, McCall zeroed in on the desk telephone. Blaine watched curiously as the Equalizer unscrewed the bowl on the telephone's receiver and proceeded to pull out a group of coloured wires. Removing a tiny pair of pliers, McCall stripped back one of the wires to reveal a thin piece of metal. The Equalizer indicated the shiny strip to the senator, who stepped closer for a better look.

'That's a descrambler,' McCall explained. 'Was the phone recently repaired?'

Blaine thought about it for a moment. 'About six months ago.'

'What kind of calls do you get on this phone?'

'Campaign stuff. Sometimes calls from the White House.'

'Any personal calls?'

'Yes,' Blaine said, growing noticeably uneasy with the Equalizer's line of questioning.

'*Very* personal?'

Blaine was reluctant to answer, but finally admitted that, yes, he had received very personal calls, as McCall was suggesting.

'What have they got on you?' the Equalizer bluntly asked him.

Blaine became suddenly less co-operative. 'I can't tell you that.'

'Blackmailers don't stop until there's nothing left,' McCall apprised him. 'When they're finished with you, they'll squeeze some other decent human being dry. Is that what you want, Senator?'

Blaine turned away abruptly, averting the Equalizer's intense glance.

'Can't you see, Mr McCall?' objected the senator. 'I don't want to discuss it any further.'

'You're playing a game with professionals. Your life could

be in danger,' McCall warned him, his tone full of genuine understanding. 'Your family could be in danger. Talk to me. I can help you.' Blaine's back remained turned to the Equalizer; he had no choice but to take a more direct approach. 'What have they got?'

Gnawing at his knuckles in frustration, Blaine wished he could avoid the Equalizer's question. But he had to face the truth: he'd been running too long, and now his troubles were getting the best of him. Weary and defeated by the situation, he moved to his desk – a man resigned to his fate. From the desktop he picked up a picture of his wife, a young, smiling dark-haired woman, and their two children, a boy and girl. The thought of losing them pained him more than he could contemplate.

'They have tapes,' he told McCall.

'Of what?'

'A questionable land deal. A tax shelter I was assured would be buried. A young girl – one of my former law students. An affair.' He reflected a moment, letting out a deep breath. 'It was all so stupid.'

'When do you have to deliver?'

'I have a number to call when I've raised a hundred thousand dollars.'

'Call it,' McCall instructed him. 'Tell them you'll make the exchange tonight on the Roosevelt Tramway. Say you'll arrange a single, special trip.'

Blaine looked at the Equalizer with amazement. How had he come up with such a plan so quickly?

The Equalizer smiled tersely. Just a routine procedure in his line of work.

Senator Blaine took the blackmailers' number out of his desk drawer as the Equalizer left the apartment. Clenching the receiver, he hesitated. Then his eye caught the picture of his wife and children again. He felt his strength gathering. This might be the toughest decision he'd ever have to make and no one, save he and this man who called himself the Equalizer, would ever be aware of it. Like a man rolling the dice in Vegas, Blaine punched the digits into the phone.

FIFTEEN

Under a bright moon which caught the glistening reflection of snow, Central Park was eerily silent. Though the evening was early yet, there were no traffic sounds, no voices. Just the rustling of frozen tree limbs scraping against each other. The trees' silhouettes cast by the moon across the snowscape moved in the breeze like dark ghosts against a linen dropcloth. The crisp sound of human footsteps punctuated the night air with a crushing sound as the Equalizer's former comrade with the Agency, Control, walked warily down a bridle path and underneath a granite footbridge. On the opposite side of the tunnel, behind the Metropolitan Museum of Art, a shadow from behind a large tree detached itself: the Equalizer. Moments later, he was walking alongside Control; the two men didn't break stride, nor did they so much as glance at each other. Control simply began talking as though continuing a conversation from another time and place.

'This is how I like to think of the park. White, sparkling,

picture-postcard. No muggers, rapists, or murderers in here tonight.'

'Just two old mercenaries taking a stroll in the moonlight. That's more dangerous.' The men finally exchanged bemused glances, then took in the view of the jewelled skyline of luxury hotels along Central Park South.

'Who gave the order to send a shadow assassin after me?' McCall asked Control.

'It came from high up,' Control responded. McCall read his expression to discern if he was telling the truth; he was. 'I've managed to bring your file down to a code-yellow violation. It's dangerous, but tolerable.'

McCall seemed surprised by Control's generosity. He knew it had taken a lot of favours for him to facilitate the change in Agency policy.

'What are the strings?'

Flashing McCall an ironic grin, Control told him, 'You can be a hero for us once in a while.'

'I can hear your sales pitch: "Why waste all that expensive training? Keep him useful. Until the day he's expendable . . ."'

'Something like that,' Control laughed wryly. 'I caught your ad.'

'And?'

'It's an interesting approach. Just make sure the odds you're trying to equalize aren't too overwhelming.'

'As a matter of fact, I'm working on some tonight.'

'Is that so?'

'Need your help.'

Control paused and glanced off towards the ancient Egyptian temple of Dendur which was illuminated behind the museum's glass wall. Agitatedly, he rubbed his hands together as if trying to warm them in the cold night air.

'This isn't quite the arrangement I had in mind.'

'It cuts both ways,' McCall reminded him. 'You'll get something out of it.'

Control considered the Equalizer's proposition. 'What do you want?'

'The Roosevelt tram.'

Control laughed. 'Is that all?'

On the other side of town, Colleen returned home from a leisurely dinner with a friend in a Columbus Avenue Italian bistro. She'd enjoyed the wine and pasta and good conversation; in fact, she realized she hadn't had a good time out for over a month. Because of the Equalizer she was able to live again like a human being – well, almost like a human being. Following his instructions, she would still have to make the phone calls to McCall's machine for a while.

After entering her apartment and securing the door behind her, Colleen pulled off her 'sleeping bag' coat and threw it on the chair. She thought about how much she missed Sarah, and how glad she would be to have her back home when life resumed its normal pattern and the terror receded into the past. Sarah was on her mind when she started for the bedroom and became aware of a gentle thumping noise which sounded like Sarah playing in the living room. It couldn't be. The next sound, that of a tiny whistle, sent chills through her.

The living room was dark, but in the glow of the streetlamp Colleen could make out Sarah's train set. Someone had very deliberately laid down the tracks on the rug and turned on the transformer. Its whistle blowing, the electric train sped around the tracks, winding its way through the *papier mâché* mountains and tunnels Colleen and Sarah had constructed together from old newspapers and glue. Circling the tracks by itself, the train and the surrounding painted terrain took on a perverse supernatural quality so startling that Colleen gasped as she came onto the bizarre scene on the living room floor.

The meaning of it was instantly clear: Steve had been here. Was here. In her apartment. Suddenly, Colleen turned to run from the apartment.

Steve's arm caught her before she could leave the room. He grabbed her around the throat. Colleen saw the glint of a knife blade flash before her eyes. She waited for its sting.

His hand covered her mouth, stifling her scream. Her eyes widened at the sight of the knife blade as he held it, the point barely touching her under her chin.

'Sorry to make you wait, baby,' Steve cooed in her ear. 'Tonight's our night.'

Roosevelt Island sat in the middle of the East River between Manhattan and the Borough of Queens. Except for the 5500 or so inhabitants who lived on the island, few New Yorkers ever ventured the three hundred yards by tram to reach the island. Once an island exile for lunatics, criminals, and incurables, the island was now residential. Only a few remnants of its past such as a dilapidated smallpox hospital were still visible.

The ride on the Swiss-built tram from Roosevelt Island to the Manhattan station at 60th Street and Second Avenue normally took three and a half minutes. Tonight it took longer.

The Equalizer arranged to meet Senator Blaine's blackmailers at the Roosevelt Island tram station. Manetti and Olsen, along with their 'security backup', Gardner boarded the tram with the Equalizer, who carried the briefcase which they believed contained their $100,000. Gardner was armed, and trained a gun on the Equalizer the moment the tram departed for Manhattan. The Equalizer made a point of guarding the briefcase which lay on the seat beside him. Inside a leather satchel, Manetti held the tapes of the conversations which could destroy Blaine.

'The catering business must be slow,' Manetti said to the Equalizer. 'I see you're moonlighting. If the Senator sent you to spy on me last night he knows more than I thought.'

'He didn't know anything. I put it together,' explained McCall to the three phone company renegades. 'Nice little operation you've got going, Manetti. Senators, corporate executives, multi-millionaires. You just sit back and listen to people hang themselves on their phones. How many of you are in on this game?'

'It's a small, exclusive circle,' Manetti grinned smugly to

himself and his cohorts, then turned to McCall. 'I hope you've brought the money.'

The Equalizer patted the briefcase beside him. 'It's right here. I went through some records today.'

'I'm sure you've found something interesting to tell me,' Manetti said sarcastically.

'You've been with the company twenty years. You're an ex-intelligence officer and a genius with communications. You were a renegade even in the Army. They never did pin that murder rap on you in Brazil.'

'No they didn't.' The smirk dissolved from Manetti's face as he got his first indication how much McCall knew of his nefarious past. 'You're full of information – classified information,' Manetti told him, feeling considerably more threatened than he had a few moments ago. 'I couldn't let you leave with all that in your head, now could I?' Manetti turned and looked out the tram window to the river below. 'It's a long way down,' he remarked, thinking how easy it would be for three men to heave McCall over the side. Convinced he had the upper hand, Manetti became demanding. 'Give us the briefcase.'

The Equalizer threw it to Olsen. Catching it, he set the briefcase on the seat, snapped open the locks, and opened the lid. Meanwhile, the Equalizer surreptitiously removed a small silver detonating device from his jacket pocket and twisted the knob at its top. His three foes were too preoccupied with the briefcase to notice McCall's secret move. When McCall triggered the blast, the blinding flash sent the three men reeling across the car. A cloud of smoke engulfed the interior of the tram.

Taking advantage of the smokescreen, the Equalizer leaped at his foe, the assassin Gardner, hitting him at the knees. As Gardner tumbled to the ground, he squeezed the trigger, but released only one shot before the Equalizer kicked the gun from his hand. The Equalizer slammed his open hand against Gardner's throat, and the assassin's neck snapped to one side.

Olsen came from behind and grabbed the Equalizer who

sensed the attack, grabbed Olsen, and sent him flying over his head. Meanwhile Manetti, lying on the floor, scrambled back to his feet and pulled a gun from his pocket. Another quick kick, and the Equalizer sent that gun flying, too; a subsequent kick took care of Manetti, connecting with his torso and sending him back into the tram wall with a heavy thud.

As Olsen regained his balance, he went for the fire extinguisher on the wall, ripped it off, and brought it down over the Equalizer's back. McCall cried out in pain, then fell to his knees, and, recovering quickly, lashed out with his legs and knocked the extinguisher from Olsen's hands. Picking himself up as fast as he had gone down, the enraged McCall hurled himself into Olsen and Manetti. Both men sprawled into a corner of the rocking tram. By catching the Equalizer off guard, Olsen got an arm around his throat and dragged him down again. Once McCall was on his stomach, Olsen jammed his knees, pinning him helplessly to the floor of the tram.

Seeing that McCall was theirs, Manetti threw the tram's emergency switch, bringing it to a dead halt. The tram rocked precariously from its cable as Manetti grabbed the glass door and slid it open. He glanced down to the river below which shone in the lights of the shoreline. At the end of Roosevelt Island, the floodlit spout of water from the Delacorte fountain gushed upwards. Bodies had been known to disappear in the fountain before; maybe McCall's would too, thought Manetti as he moved towards Olsen's hostage.

Then without warning the Equalizer broke Olsen's grasp, whirling him around and throwing him towards the wall of the tram. This time there was no wall to break his fall. Olsen went sailing out the open doorway, down to the river below. Lunging at the emergency switch, the Equalizer threw the handle forward and started the tram moving again. His hand still on the switch, McCall's eye caught Manetti diving for his fallen gun. The Equalizer got there first, kicked it away, then threw himself at Manetti, who wriggled out from under his grasp. The tram pitched violently in the struggle between the two men, causing Manetti to roll toward the open doorway. Just when he was certain that Manetti was headed for a watery grave in the East River, McCall saw Manetti's hand catch the side of the door. Breaking his fall, Manetti climbed up the outside of the door, pulling himself upward towards the roof of the tram. From the door, he hoisted himself to the roof of the tram where he hoped he could better escape from McCall.

The Equalizer went after Manetti. As Manetti reached the roof of the tram, McCall grabbed a hold of the outside of the door and began pulling himself towards the roof. Already standing on top of the tram, Manetti looked down to see the Equalizer's hand curling over the top of the doorway. With his heavy shoe, he attempted to stomp on McCall's hand; instead, the Equalizer caught his foot, twisted it, and threw him backwards. Manetti hit the metal roof of the tram with a resounding bang. Desperately, he reached for the machinery atop the tram to prevent him from rolling off.

The tram had crossed the river and was now passing over the island of Manhattan, coming into the 60th Street station. The two men continued to grapple, rolling dangerously close to the edge of the car. Their hands flailed wildly, grabbing at anything that would prevent them from falling or allowing the opponent to get the advantage. Manetti went for the Equalizer's throat. In a swift move, he threw himself onto McCall and brought his cupped hands down at his face. But the Equalizer twisted at the last moment. Manetti's hands smashed down onto metal. The tram pitched to the side, still swinging on its cable as it moved ever nearer the station. Thrown off balance, Manetti slipped and rolled over the roof of the tram. His hands unavailingly groped for anything that could save him – but found nothing.

The Equalizer saw the flash of Manetti's hand as it went over the side of the car and disappeared into the darkness below. Manetti's fading scream was carried off by the howl of the wind through the city streets. Lying still atop the tram, the Equalizer, exhausted from his struggle, gasped for breath.

Moments later, the tram smoothly glided into the 60th Street Station just as it usually did on its regular run, with one exception: the Equalizer could be seen climbing down from its roof and jumping to the floor of the car. Control was there on the platform waiting for him; with him were two other agents, Anson and Hellman, forming a welcoming committee. McCall wasn't especially pleased to see them.

'I'll take the tapes, Robert,' Control greeted McCall as he stepped of the tram.

The Equalizer wouldn't honour Hellman or Anson with a glance. 'I lost two of them coming over,' he informed Control. 'One was Manetti. He was running his own cell within the phone company. There's still one of them, a hitman, inside the tram.' The agents looked at the unconscious Gardner sprawled on the floor. McCall's look begged understanding from the impassive Control. 'You could destroy those tapes on Blaine.'

Control deliberated, then retorted, 'No. *You* could. I have to function within the confines of the bureaucratic machinery you hate so much. The tapes will be turned over to a Senate committee.'

'You know what that'll do to Blaine.'

Yes, he was well aware it would end the senator's Presidential bid, and perhaps his political career also. 'I know,' Control replied regretfully, but didn't believe he had any other choice in the matter. 'If I need you . . .'

'You know where to find me.'

McCall and Control held on each other's eyes for a moment. Then McCall walked slowly out of the tram station.

SIXTEEN

Colleen sat pressed against her couch. Her hands were tied. The terror had only just begun.

She had held her breath while Steve cut the buttons of her blouse, one by one, relishing her agony as she squirmed underneath him. Now he was sitting opposite her. His legs were crossed. The knife point was inches away from Colleen's throat. She dared not scream or utter a sound. She tried not to cry, but the tears came anyway, running down her throat into her cleavage. Sitting still, her back rigid, she took the tears off her face, afraid to so much as move her hands. She had never felt so helpless or doomed in her life. The thought of rape was bad enough, but now she was almost certain that rape wouldn't be enough for the psychotic young man – he would kill her. She would never see her daughter again. Sarah would have to grow up without a mother. In a moment of relative clarity, Colleen had the thought that if she could appease her attacker somehow, give the impression she was co-operating, then he might spare her life. It was a chance, and even if she survived, she would have to live with the horror of the rape the rest of her life. But at least she would live.

'Come on. Get it over with,' she calmly demanded. 'I'm not going to beg. I'm not going to scream. I'm not going to do anything. Do what you want. But just do it.'

She held still a moment, anticipating his reaction, all the while hoping her approach would satisfy him.

Suddenly Steve reared back his hand and with the full force of his arm slapped her across the face. The brunt of his hand on her face stunned her. It wasn't what she was expecting, and it had an altogether different effect on her. It jarred her out of her submission. The blow unleashed her defiance, and Colleen launched herself from the couch at her assailant, ramming into him and knocking him over. She saw the knife clatter to the floor, and Steve reaching for it.

Please God, she thought to herself, let me get it before he does.

But another noise distracted her, the sound of the front door bursting open and banging against the wall. In that split second of distraction, Steve regained his bearings and went for the knife. She heard a familiar voice, the Equalizer's, calling from the hallway.

'Colleen!'

'Here,' she shouted, crawling away from Steve.

There wasn't time for her to get away. Steve had the knife again, and Colleen was within striking distance. Like a cornered animal, Steve would attack without hesitating and – though Colleen didn't know it – her screams only drove him closer to the brink of complete madness. His eyes had a killer's intensity. The boyishness was absent from his face, which in the streetlight's amber glow had the look of a hellish fiend.

The Equalizer ran down the short hallway into the living room, his gun in hand.

'I'll cut her throat,' Steve told him as he came to an abrupt stop in a stand-off in the living room.

Shielding his body with Colleen's, Steve held her tightly

against him. The knife was a steel line across the front of her throat, capable of cutting her with only the slightest move.

Immediately sizing up the peril before him, the Equalizer flashed back to that night at Grand Central. His mind replayed the image of the station platform, the knife raised, Carolides shouting, 'I'll cut her throat.' Now he was reliving that moment, and it gave him pause.

Then Steve, intoxicated by the life-and-death control he wielded, began to giggle. Sensing in him the weakness of a lunatic, Colleen wrenched free of his grasp. The instant she removed herself from the Equalizer's line of fire, McCall shot from the hip, just as he had that night on the station platform.

The bullet's impact knocked Steve backwards. The knife dropped from his hand to the floor. He stared curiously at his arm and the blood running down it from the wound in his chest. He fell to the floor, moving for the last time.

McCall reached down and picked up the fallen knife. Colleen sobbed uncontrollably. She looked away, unable to bear the sight of the rapist's body lying on her living room floor amid the wreckage of her daughter's toys. The Equalizer gently came up behind her and turned her towards him; with the knife, he cut her bonds. As she continued to convulse with sobs, the Equalizer pulled her towards him and held her tightly as if she were his own daughter.

'It's all over now . . .'

The Equalizer had one more promise to keep that evening – a date at the High School of Performing Arts.

The concert was in progress and nearing the end of the final strains of Beethoven's Fifth Symphony. The small orchestra of students filled the hall with a giant sound. The packed auditorium sat rapt with attention. Janice McCall, in one of the front rows, stared proudly at her son Scott as his fingers and bow moved at an allegro tempo over the violin. Throughout the concert, she had been all too aware of the empty seat beside her. She should have known better than to take Robert at his word that he would show. It was one thing to lead *her* on, but to do it to Scott . . .

Then she noticed someone moving along the side of the auditorium and standing against the wall down front. Taking her eyes away from the stage, she saw Robert and smiled. Well, it was good of him to come, even if the concert was nearly over. He had kept his promise to Scott. He had made it after all.

McCall watched his son perform with a father's awe and adoration. The Beethoven overwhelmed him as it never had before. The thought of his son mastering the complex music was almost beyond the Equalizer's comprehension. The soaring strains of the notes ringing through the concert hall were an antidote to the ugliness out there in the world against which McCall had to struggle day to day. This was beauty, and love, in its purest form.

When the orchestra let loose with the resounding final notes of the symphony, the audience burst into tumultuous applause. The old European conductor, maestro Marvin Einhorn, even seemed pleased with the results of his student orchestra. He exited into the wings, returning to take a bow as the orchestra rose from their seats. Along with the others on stage, Scott bowed forward as the applause washed over them in waves. Ecstasy was written all over his face. Squinting, he looked into the lights and searched the audience and found his father, standing along the wall and applauding wildly.

Scott spoke softly to himself, smiling contentedly. 'He did make it.'

The audience rose in a standing ovation. Still clapping his hands, the Equalizer returned his son's smile, then glanced across the auditorium to Janice, who was on her feet with the rest of the audience. Feeling his eyes on her, she looked over at the Equalizer and mouthed the words, 'Thank you. I love you.'

The Equalizer winked back at her as the applause rang on. When the Equalizer returned to the New York Café and restaurant the following evening, he felt somewhat sluggish, suddenly aware how much the events over the past few days had drained him.

As he walked over to Carol at the bar, the 'News at Eleven' came on the TV set above the bar. The announcer rattled off the details of the phone company scandal which had reached into the corridors of the nation's Capitol, forever affecting the life and career of Senator James Blaine. McCall listened to the story, aware of all the details and hoping the media would spare Blaine pain and embarrassment. If Control had shown mercy, the worst of the scandal would never come to light.

McCall watched the screen intently as the anchorman switched to a correspondent stationed at Blaine's New York headquarters. The crowd looked considerably restrained in sharp contrast to the rally the Equalizer had attended there. Blaine's young, patrician wife, Elizabeth Ellison Blaine stood by her husband, as did their two children, Patrick and Letha. Obviously nervous, his voice full of emotion, Blaine stepped to the microphone to address the TV cameras and his campaign loyalists.

When the cheering crowd quietened, sensing what was about to come, Blaine began to read. 'Thank you, thank you. At this time I'd like to read from a prepared statement,' he said, taking a pair of glasses from his pocket. Putting on the glasses, he seemed significantly older; the ordeal already having taken its toll on the senator's youthful looks. He spoke solemnly:

'To my devoted supporters, constituents, people of the United States, and ladies and gentlemen of the press: It is with regret, for personal reasons, that I must step down and decline the Democratic nomination for the Presidency of the United States.'

Without further ado or questions, he withdrew from the microphones, taking the hands of his wife and children and moving down the podium steps in a flurry of flashbulbs. Meanwhile his disappointed supporters offered up a last hurrah for the shaken candidate.

Carol, noting the news, greeted the Equalizer. 'It's a shame, huh?'

The Equalizer nodded. He felt Blaine's disappointment and hurt personally. The man was so young and idealistic; had shown so much promise. And then this . . .

'There's a fella waiting for you over by the window,' said Carol, interrupting the Equalizer's thoughts.

McCall thanked her, turned, and moved over to the table which appeared to be perched on the edge of the UN Building. Hamilton was there waiting for him. Relaxed, he sipped a glass of wine, then rose as the Equalizer approached.

'I'm celebrating. I got my job back today.'

'Congratulations.'

'Guess you've seen the papers. But none of them mention you.'

'They won't.'

Hamilton took a cheque from his pocket and handed it to the Equalizer. 'Thank you.'

McCall took the cheque and, without bothering to read the amount payable, stuffed it in his coat pocket. Hamilton shook his hand, gave him a look of gratitude, and left the restaurant. McCall was watching him go when proprietor John Perry diverted his attention.

'There's that young lady waiting for you at the last booth,' he informed McCall. 'She doesn't seem to be so shaken up tonight.'

'Thanks, Johnny.'

The Equalizer slid into the booth opposite Colleen. Despite what John Perry had told him, her hands were still shaking, and she tried to calm them by clasping them together.

She smiled up at McCall. 'Sorry. I can't stop them from trembling.'

'They'll stop,' McCall said, giving her a reassuring smile, and added, more seriously, 'I owe you an apology. I misread Steve. I thought I'd scared him away. What I did was push him over the edge. That's why he came back for you.'

Colleen gently touched the Equalizer's hand.

'You don't owe me anything,' she told him softly. 'I owe you. How do you thank the man who saved your life?'

'You just did.'

Apparently, she didn't think the thanks were adequate. She opened her purse, took out an envelope, and offered it to McCall.

'I withdrew my savings,' she told him. 'A thousand dollars. I know your fee must be very high, but . . .'

He interrupted her quietly, saying, 'The fee is a hundred dollars.'

She thought her ears were deceiving her. No one in these modern times, in New York no less, could be so altruistic. Incredulous, she stared at him, then did as he asked and placed a hundred dollar bill into his hand. He pocketed the bill while she continued:

'Last night was the first time I was able to sleep in two months.' He was glad for her and, taking her remark as a compliment, smiled graciously. With some hesitation, she awkwardly posed a different sort of question. 'I wondered whether you'd come to dinner one night?'

'I'll have to pass,' he said matter-of-factly.

She didn't want to take 'no' for an answer. 'I'd like to get to know you better.'

'No you wouldn't,' he told her gently, thinking of his wife, son, his work, and all the loose ends in his life of late. 'Not yet.'

Colleen was plainly disappointed, but did nothing to try to disguise it. 'Will I ever see you again?'

The Equalizer slid out of the booth and stood up.

'If you've ever got a problem,' he smiled, 'you know the number to call.'

Her eyes were on his back as he walked away from her towards the restaurant's exit. Too quietly for him to hear, she said, 'Good-bye, Mr McCall.'

He left the restaurant, took the elevator to the building's lobby, and sauntered across the avenue towards the UN. The snow had begun to melt, and he side-stepped the dark slush on the street and sidewalk. Glancing upward, he paused, took a breath of the fine, cold air, and gazed in a kind of wonder at the blazing lights of the box-like United Nations offices and the round General Assembly. By all rights, his years of intelligence work and adversary relationships in the world of cloak and dagger diplomacy should have inured him to the ideals the United Nations represented. But, dwarfed by the magnificence of the structure and the things it symbolized, he couldn't help being moved. He had the sudden notion that its purpose and his were the same, and that his affinity for the building was more than accidental.

As he had hoped would happen when he packed his bags to leave Washington, his own sense of purpose had been restored in New York. Much lay ahead to be experienced. But challenges and problems weren't interruptions in the Equalizer's life; they were the essence of it. Everything in life was resolved eventually, one way or the other. He had taken the first steps towards resolving the unanswered questions in his own existence. A free man owned by no one and owing to nothing save his own conscience, McCall had discovered a degree of satisfaction in his work he had only ever dreamt of finding before. Being a mercenary out of one's own moral convictions felt considerably different from being a mercenary out of someone else's expedient, morally questionable policy.

Strolling along the railing beside the East River, he gazed beyond the dark water to the orange neon lights of the old Silvercup bakery on the opposite shore. Ignoring the cold, McCall examined his actions of the past few days, actions which would soon be distant memories. But he would never forget how he felt at this moment. His body tingled with sensations of renewal. And as he followed the water flowing towards the Atlantic, an inner glow swept through him. This was what life was about.

He held the things that mattered before him in the looking glass of his mind's eye.

The Equalizer knew he had truly come home.

SEVENTEEN

Scott McCall gazed out of the windows of his father's apartment down to the sunny street below. The snow that had blanketed the city only a week before was gone. It was an unseasonably warm, late autumn day. People dressed in no more than shirt sleeves were out walking their dogs, sitting on their stoops, conversing with neighbours, and jogging to the rhythms of their Walkman audio cassettes. Scott glanced around his dad's living room. The place was starkly white, especially in the bright sunshine. He could feel the warmth penetrating his High School of the Performing Arts sweatshirt. Too warm, he took it off and draped it over the white couch.

Robert McCall was happily engaged across the room at the open kitchen counter. Slicing off bits of turkey, he carefully arranged them atop bread, tomato and lettuce. Scott could see the pleasure he was getting from preparing the simple lunch. He wanted to keep the occasion casual, but no matter what he did, his dad worked at making it a special event. He tried to relax and just let his dad enjoy the day. But he couldn't. It wasn't natural to be with him, at least not yet; Scott wondered if it ever would be.

'Mustard or mayo?' his father asked.

'Neither,' Scott replied. McCall topped off his sandwich with the toasted bread and sliced it as Scott made light conversation. 'Your place looks great since you got everything out of the boxes.'

McCall reached into the refrigerator and shouted out, 'I've rearranged the back bedroom. It's yours for weekends, perhaps. It will give us a chance to spend some time together.'

Scott turned to his father as he returned to the kitchen counter. 'I'm leaving the city,' he blurted out; immediately he wished he could have couched it more softly.

Stepping into the living room with the sandwiches in hand, McCall was caught off guard. 'Oh!' he exclaimed, obviously distressed by the news and trying to disguise it.

'I've been accepted at the Strasbourg Conservatory in Paris.'

McCall looked proudly at his son, and was filled with a rush of pride at his accomplishment. The Strasbourg Conservatory ranked among the best in the world. Scott's acceptance was a measure of his maturity and artistry as a violinist.

'That's quite an honour,' he said matter-of-factly, downplaying it because Scott had. 'But I'm not surprised. You have worked very hard.' Scott expected his father to drop the plates of sandwiches and embrace him; he was surprised Dad took it so calmly. 'When do you leave?' his father asked.

'Tuesday.'

Again, McCall was taken aback and clearly showed it. 'That soon?' Scott nodded. 'How long will you be gone?'

'A year at least. But if I like them and, more importantly, if they like me, it could be longer.'

Though it wasn't easy for him to admit to his feelings, Robert McCall confessed to his disappointment which tempered the pride he felt for Scott.

'This catches me a little off guard,' he told him candidly. 'I was hoping that, well, part of the reason that I moved to New York was for us to be able to spend time together.'

Scott was direct with his father, though it hurt him to let his dad down. 'I just can't pass it up.'

'I wasn't suggesting that. Of course you can't.' McCall pondered the situation for a moment. 'Tuesday,' he said, thinking, then offered a suggestion. 'Then let's take these days – this weekend.'

'I'd like to,' Scott began, stammering, 'but . . . but . . . there's so much to do. I have to finish packing, and . . .'

McCall set the sandwiches on the counter and stepped forward to his son. He wouldn't beg, but his emotional need to be with Scott was clearly evident in his eyes. 'Two days, Scott,' he said plaintively. 'Just two days. We'll get out of the city. Some place interesting. And just . . .'

Scott turned away, his resentment against his father taking him in its grip. Scott knew that his father needed him, badly, and that he might get some petty satisfaction from withholding himself from his father's company. He fought his instinct to get back at his father for all the times McCall had abandoned him.

'But of course, I understand,' McCall rambled, letting Scott off the hook. 'You have a lot to do before you leave.'

Scott wasn't responding. McCall thought for a moment and realized he was evading the real issue of emotional intimacy with his son. He refused to avoid it any more, to let wounds fester, to make up for the past in some distant future. In his new life, he had no choice but to tell Scott exactly how he felt and what he wanted from their relationship.

'There were just some things I wanted to say,' McCall told his son. 'Things which need the proper setting.'

Scott understood what his father had on his mind. He sympathized with his father's distress, and shared his inability to articulate the wealth of unverbalized emotions which lay under the surface, forming a barrier between them. Anger and hate were emotions he could never bring himself to admit to; but then, so were love and need. Though some thirty years separated father and son, neither had accepted his own human feelings and ceased to be ashamed of them. It gave Scott no solace to know that a man he respected as much as his father was capable of being stuck in the same emotional quagmire as his teenage son. Just as the elder McCall had the maturity to know these emotions would be resolved, Scott had a maturity of another sort – the maturity to know that, while things might not get better, they could not go on as they were. Something had to give. Unless he made himself available to his father, nothing would ever change.

'All right,' Scott said to his father. 'You want the weekend – you got it.'

The Equalizer nodded gratefully, showing to his son none of the happiness which welled up inside.

The next morning, Scott threw his clothes for the weekend into a duffel bag. His mother Janice watched him pack hastily for the trip with his father. Although she would have been elated under most circumstances for Scott to spend time with his father, she wished they'd picked another weekend. This would be the last time she would have with Scott for a while, too, and she was feeling the pangs of having her son, grown into young manhood, leave home.

Scott was waiting in front of his building when his dad's Jaguar pulled up. He threw his bag into the back seat, and they were off through mid-town Manhattan and bound for the country. Scott was silent as they sped along the river's FDR drive, past the slums of East Harlem, and headed for the Tri-Borough Bridge which would take them out of Manhattan. Scott was quiet as the city slid by outside the car window; finally, as they crossed the East River, he asked his father, 'This cabin we're going to – how did you arrange it so quickly?'

'I used it once.'

'What for?'

'To keep a man safe.'

'A spy?'

McCall chuckled at Scott's question, but avoided an answer all the same.

'Who's side?' he asked his father, not letting the issue of the spy die.

McCall was absorbed in his driving, manoeuvring into another lane for the Bronx interchange. 'What?'

'Was he on our side or theirs?'

McCall chuckled again, this time at the way Scott posed the question. 'Those words – that question is for novels. There are so many "ours" and so many different "theirs", and all so interchangeable that then he was "theirs" but now he would be "ours".'

'Sounds crazy,' commented Scott in earnest.

'It was crazy,' McCall laughed, seeing the absurdity of government politics in a new light now that he was no longer a part of the system. 'And it's still crazy.'

'And did you – did you keep him safe?'

McCall dropped the levity and became suddenly very serious as he glanced at his son.

'No.'

The memory of it still stung the Equalizer. He pushed harder on the accelerator. The Jaguar shot forward, making a quick pass through the Bronx until they were heading into the country, up the Hutchinson River Parkway through Westchester county. Though out of the city for barely half an hour, the tree-lined parkway, old stone bridges, country houses, and small towns along the route made the landscape appear to be hours away from New York City. The sun continued to shine brightly on browning autumn leaves which still clung to their branches after the early snow. Scott rolled down the window and inhaled the aroma of leaves burning in small bonfires. The sunlight, meandering between the tree branches, made dappled patterns on the Jaguar's windscreen as they drove through the harvest golds of the countryside.

Scott considered his father's answer, and took it as an

105

indication that maybe this time McCall would be different and be open with him.

'You've never talked about your "job" before,' Scott pointed out. 'Usually when I asked that kind of question, all I would get back would be mumbles. Why the change?'

'It is important this weekend that we are both candid – about everything. It's the only chance for you to get to know me, and for me to get to know you. I want that very much, Scott, and there isn't much time.'

His anger triggered by his father's remark, Scott flew into a rage. All the years of bottled-up pain popped out, the pain suddenly fresh again, as if it were only yesterday his father had rejected him for his shadow life of service in the government.

'No!' Scott exploded. 'Not now! *Now* there's not much time. But whose fault is that?'

The outburst was not like Scott, thought McCall. His son had always been calm, polite, occasionally moody; but not openly furious. Seeing Scott's face flush with rage, McCall pulled the car over to a sudden stop near a cross road. Scott didn't bother to wait for the Jaguar to come to a complete halt, preferring instead to bail out while it was still moving.

There wasn't much traffic at the country crossroads. There wasn't much around either – just an antique store with a lot of junk hanging from the eaves and a rusted horse-drawn sleigh out front. The light traffic on the highway sped by without paying much attention to McCall and Scott. The Equalizer jumped out of the car and confronted his son who stood on the shoulder of the road.

'You want to whip me about the past?' McCall demanded to know. 'Is that what this weekend is going to be?'

'Hey, I wish we had a past!' retorted Scott angrily.

It was clear that both McCall the elder and McCall the younger, similarly stubborn, were each going to stand their ground, neither acquiescing to the other, neither taking any verbal abuse or humiliation. The two glowered at each other for a moment, holding back for fear of hurting each other more than they already had. McCall's eyes softened as Scott held his look; then, without saying a word, Scott strode quickly to the driver's side and got in. McCall remained standing on the shoulder until Scott yelled through the open passenger door.

'I'll drive.'

McCall smiled slightly at the way Scott was trying to redefine their roles by switching places. If Scott wanted to have the experience of being in control, McCall would let him. Real emotional growth, he knew from experience, came from relinquishing control when necessary, not fighting to keep it.

'Are you impugning my driving ability?' asked McCall, still standing outside the car.

Scott's mouth betrayed a trace of a smile. 'What ability?'

McCall ambled over to the passenger side and got into the seat. 'If this is an indication of this weekend, maybe we should just go back right now.'

'Go back?' laughed Scott, putting the car in gear. 'No. That would be too easy. And the last thing I want this weekend to be is easy.'

McCall would have laughed, but he knew that – even if Scott were joking – he really meant it.

EIGHTEEN

King's Harbor, Maine, had the sort of small-town ram-shackle, quaintness and Americana of a Norman Rockwell illustration. The town of fifteen hundred residents boasted one main street, much of which was already closed for the season, or just plain closed. Folks here were open for business when they felt like it. Everybody knew everybody else, or was related, their families going back several generations. There wasn't a newspaper, as such, but King's Harbor didn't really need one. Most of the news was spread by gossip, and the hub of the grapevine was Ye Olde General Store – which lived up to its name by virtue of not having been painted in fifteen years.

A town like King's Harbor didn't see many Jaguars. So people took notice when Scott drove his father's car down the main street of town. Heads began turning as far up the road as the Angler's Inn, which had been around since 1790. A pair of old, pot-bellied men were rocking conten-tedly in their rocking chairs on the inn's porch when they saw that 'fancy foreign automobile' zip past. Scott drove on down the road, past a shattered Dairy Queen, a parking lot boasting one rusted junker pickup truck, and a one-pump gas station where two pimple-faced teenagers loitered about drinking a soda. Heads may have turned at the sight of the Jaguar, but few thought much more about it beyond that.

Scott pulled the car into the gas station, which sat across the street from the bait and tackle shop and Ye Old General Store. A gum-chewing, lanky teenager who resembled a slovenly young Abe Lincoln filled the Jaguar with gas. Scott got out, stretched his legs, and leaned against the car, looking across to the General Store. Underneath the faded sign, was a smaller, more recent sign which read 'Co-op Grocery'. McCall crossed the street to get some groceries.

Moments later, Scott looked across the way at the store again. Standing in front of the grey, weatherbeaten building was a cute, fragile-looking girl who appeared to be about Scott's age. She was sporting sunglasses, cheap earrings, a halter top, and fun jewellery in a variety of bright day-glo colours. Melinda looked like a refugee from the punk and art scene in Manhattan's East Village. One thing was certain: she didn't belong in a sleepy fishing village in Maine. Beside her, sitting on his battered rucksack, was her travelling companion Jake, who got tired of hearing people say he looked like James Dean; he wished people would think of something more original to say. When they met while hitchhiking, Melinda had told him he looked like Matt Dillon. That's when they'd become friends. At the moment, they were weary from life on the road; it had been a long wait since their last ride. Glancing Scott across the way, Melinda picked up her hand-lettered sign – *BOSTON* – and flashed it at Scott.

Scott read the sign, smiled, and regretfully shook his head. Running his finger down from his eye, he mimed tears of disappointment and put his hand to his heart. Melinda gave him a small smile, then tried again, flipping the sign over to flash: *TORONTO*. Scott laughed and shrugged to indicate that he wasn't headed for Canada either.

McCall, a bag of groceries in hand along with the set of keys to the cabin, emerged from the store. Scott paid the gas station attendant. Pulling away from the pump in the Jaguar, Scott kept an eye on Melinda in his rear-view mirror as she receded into the distance.

Slumping down onto the ground, Melinda watched, disappointed, while the departing Jag disappeared. There wasn't a sign of another car anywhere on the road.

'It was dumb taking that last ride,' Melinda chided Jake. 'We should have stayed on the main road.'

'I said I'm sorry,' Jake said testily.

'Jake, I'm not accusing you.'

He shot her an annoyed look. 'No, you just see fit to mention it every ten minutes,' he said facetiously.

'Well, I just think it was stupid.'

'And it was my idea, but you're not accusing me.'

Frustrated, she picked up a rock and hurled it against a building post. 'Forget it.'

'I'm trying to,' he said, staring angrily ahead.

'You know, you're really a jerk sometimes,' she told him. 'You're just so . . . defensive. I can't handle it.'

'Then don't,' he replied, scrambling to his feet and brushing himself off. 'I'm gonna get something to drink.'

Grabbing his rucksack, Jake started to walk back into the store. He stopped in his tracks at the sound of an approaching truck. It was a four by four crew cab pickup, all shiny and black with yellow trim. A roll bar extended across the top of the truck, and a brace of tungsten lights were affixed to the roof of the cab. The sound of the truck roaring out of a side street onto the highway put Melinda on the alert. With a reflex reaction, she raised the sign. But as soon as she got a look at the truck, she changed her mind and instinctively lowered the sign just as quickly as she'd raised it. Meanwhile Jake had his thumb out for a ride.

The truck sped past both of them, and Melinda wondered if she'd done the right thing by passing up what could prove their only shot at a lift. Then the truck slid to a dusty stop as the driver slammed on the brakes. Melinda and Jake watched as the truck just sat there. The motor continued to rumble; the dust settled around the tyres. Melinda wasn't sure it was stopping for them. Maybe the guys had forgotten to pick up some groceries and stopped because they'd suddenly remembered. Then again, maybe they were deciding among themselves whether to offer her and Jake a ride.

The truck roared backwards like a dragster coming off the line. Its engine continued to race, and its big nobby wheels sprayed dust and dirt everywhere. Taken by surprise, Melinda and Jake exchanged startled glances and jumped back out of the way as the truck skidded to a stop.

The dust around the pickup settled. The face of a young country boy, Dillart, popped out of the window and grinned at the pair of hitchhikers with a lopsided grin.

'Where are you goin'?' Dillart asked in a distinct Maine accent. While Dillart hung out of the window of the truck, his pals Bobby, the driver, and Ray, sitting in the back seat, guzzled bottles of beer. The three of them seemed innocent enough to Jake, who was ready to jump at the chance of a ride. But Melinda had misgivings. So what if they were young, fresh, handsome, and athletic? They were boozing it up on a Saturday afternoon and riding around looking for some action to break the boredom of this hick town. She didn't want any part of them.

'We're headed for Boston, then Toronto' she said, in response to Dillart's question.

Bobby, the driver, leaned across the front seat and yelled out the window. 'We got room for one.'

His friends in the back seat laughed uproariously.

'Just kiddin', Dillart assured Melinda, and opened the door in mock gentlemanly fashion. 'Throw your stuff in the back.'

'That's all right,' said Melinda. 'We're kind of waiting for a straight shot – one ride all the way.'

'You'll never get it,' Bobby interjected. 'Not in this neck of the woods.'

Sensing she was desperate and vulnerable, Dillart nudged her, trying to convince her. 'Come on. We'll drop you at the interstate.'

'No,' said Melinda, sticking with her instincts. 'Thanks anyway, but . . .'

'What the hell,' Ray piped up from the back of the pickup, 'you too good to take a ride from us?'

Dillart smiled the kind of broad, inviting smile Melinda would expect from the boy-next-door. 'Come on. We're harmless. Besides, Bobby's right. You'll be here till sun-up waiting for a ride.'

Melinda and Jake looked at each other as they tried to determine what to do. Then they glanced down the winding highway surrounded by pine trees – a million miles from anywhere and not a car in sight. Shrugging his shoulders, Jake caved in. 'We would have a better chance at the interstate,' he argued, sensing that Melinda was weakening.

Aware of her vulnerability, Dillart reached down, picked up her bag, and threw it in the back of the truck. 'It's on our way.'

Melinda, still uneasy and convinced that she had no alternatives, climbed in the truck. The three raucous young men let loose with a welcoming cheer as she clambered aboard with her friend Jake.

'All right,' Bobby shouted gleefully, waving his bottle of beer and then chugging the rest of it down.

'Kick this pig in the butt, Bobby,' shouted Ray. 'Let's see what the Harley will do.'

The doors slammed. The engine roared. Kicking up dust, the truck shot out onto the highway. Bobby pitched his empty beer bottle out of the window and grabbed another cold beer. Squeezed in between the men, Melinda was already uncomfortable. She felt trapped, as though they were deliberately snaring her and awaiting their moment to pounce. Dillart shoved a beer in her face. She declined. Jake took one just to be one of the boys, but even he had the gnawing feeling in his gut that he and Melinda should have taken their chances back at the general store.

Scott didn't think they could get any deeper into the woods without losing the road. A few turns in from the local highway, past a couple of secluded farms, the pavement gave way to gravel, and then to dirt. The Jaguar kicked up a trail of dust in its wake. Scott slowed to avoid ruts in the road eroded by the recent rains and snow. Suddenly driving wasn't as much fun as it was on the winding parkways on the way up from New York. Scott just hoped his father's car had sturdy shock absorbers; he'd hate to see the repair bill on a Jag for demolished shocks. McCall assured him that the car would survive undamaged; there wasn't much ground to cover before they arrived at the cabin. Scott hoped his father was right. He was.

The cabin fitted Scott's image of an old gold prospector's retreat somewhere high up in the Sierra Nevada mountain range. It was nestled amid the thick evergreen forest, completely surrounded by foliage except for its front, which opened onto the cow path that masqueraded as a road. The walls had been hewn of logs. It was hard to say when. Maybe five years ago. Maybe a hundred. One thing was obvious – no one had used it in a long time. The cabin was a victim of neglect, gloomy, overgrown with weeds on its porch, covered with debris on the roof, cracked window panes, a screen door off its hinges.

The sight of it awed Scott. After he parked the car in front of the rickety porch, he paused in wonder at the retreat to which his father had brought him. No outside world to interfere with them here. They'd be like a couple of monks communing with God. Finally Scott stirred from his state of amazement, got out of the driver's seat, and slowly approached the front door. Meanwhile, his dad went to the back of the car to retrieve their bags from the trunk.

Taking the keys his father had given him, Scott unlocked the door and held his breath in the presence of their dilapidated one-room abode. Because the windows were shuttered, and because Scott's eyes weren't adjusted to the darkness, it was difficult for him to make out the interior at first. Not knowing where to find the light switch, he took a flashlight from his overnight bag just in case he'd need it to see. From what he could discern, the furnishings consisted of a rocking chair, some smaller wooden chairs, a crude table holding an old, dusty telephone, two empty paraffin lamps, a refrigerator, and an ancient wooden stove. Along the walls he spied something which looked like two single beds. In keeping with the rustic decor, someone had provided an enormous set of elk antlers as interior decoration; these hung as a centrepiece in the room, like a coat rack directly over the rough stone fireplace.

'Very homey,' Scott said to his father as he came behind him through the door. The outside light cut a swathe across the floor to the fireplace. Scott set his things down on the hearth and checked the flashlight. It wasn't working. Cupping his hands over its lens, he discovered the bulb was barely glowing.

'There goes the flashlight,' he told his father. 'It's been on the whole time.' He turned it off, though he doubted that would do much good. McCall casually hung his overcoat on one of the huge elk antlers which worked better as a coat rack than they did as ornamentation.

Scott went outside and strolled around the cabin. Whoever had built the place had made it small, solid, and basic. There were shuttered windows in the front and on the sides, and two doors, a front and a back entrance. The shutters would be enough to keep prowlers out during the off-season when no one was there; that is, if prowlers could find their way into this part of the forest. On a second look, the cabin was more inviting. The sounds of birds and the wind through the trees filled the air. Scott jammed his hands into his pockets, closed his eyes, and took a deep breath of the country smells. He exhaled. He could feel some of the tension leaving his body. The place brought back fond memories of his childhood.

'Pretty radical place,' he told his father as he emerged from inside the cabin. 'Reminds me a lot of Tamackwa.'

'Tamackwa?' McCall ruminated lightly, teasing. 'I hear they can treat that now.'

'It was a camp I went to when we lived in Connecti-cut . . . Mum and I.'

McCall became very quiet, taking his son's remark as a dig at him. Not knowing how to respond, he bowed his head and tried to think of something. Scott picked up on his father's uneasiness.

'I didn't mean it like that,' he said apologetically.

McCall shook his head and looked Scott squarely in the eye. 'Scott, if there's a way we can learn to treat each other with kid gloves off, I'd like to find it. If we keep on like this, we'll never get a chance to find out what we really feel about one another. And that would be the saddest part . . . to only have fragmented memories to take with us when you leave next Tuesday.'

Scott shuffled his feet in the dirt; looked uncomfortably at his running shoes. 'So how does it work?' he asked, eager to find another approach to solving their communication problems. 'How do we shift gears here?'

'I think it starts with me acting like a father without having any guilt about it.'

Scott smiled and in a tone somewhat like Groucho Marx quipped, 'That sounds vaguely foreboding.'

Feigning sternness, McCall gave him an order: 'Unpack those bags and clean up the cabin.'

And Scott, rebounding from the cue, acted the role of a movie director directing an actor: 'A little more severe!'

'Unpack those bags and clean up the cabin,' McCall reiterated – a little more severe in accordance with his son's directions.

Scott smiled again. 'You're on your way.'

Cheerful, Scott bounded into the cabin to unpack his bags and clean up the place.

NINETEEN

'Excuse the pigs,' said Dillart, stifling an obnoxious laugh as Ray, offering a beer to Melinda, spilled it down the front of her blouse. Wedged between Dillart and Bobby in the back seat of the truck cab, she couldn't very well evade the obviously intentional spill. Her face screwed up in disgust at Ray.

'Let me wipe it off,' volunteered Bobby, reaching for Melinda's ample breasts, which were ever more pronounced under the wet fabric.

'That's all right,' she said, and pushed his hand away with annoyance. 'I don't need any help.'

Ray took another swallow of beer and wiped his mouth with the back of his hand. He reeked of sweat and the sickly sweet smell of malt. Melinda regarded him with even greater revulsion as he leaned in very close to her ear and whispered loudly, 'You two a set or what?' He indicated Jake with a nod.

'Just friends,' she replied curtly. She twisted her head to avoid the horrible smell of his thick breath.

Ray rolled his eyes towards Bobby, who knew what his buddy was thinking: Melinda was fair game. They had themselves a live one – if they could just get her to play along and enjoy the fun. The boyfriend would have to co-operate; then again, if he didn't, there were ways to handle that, too.

'Want a beer, bub?' Ray asked Jake, extending another bottle. Jake had had his fill, of the beer and of this company. He wished he and Melinda had heeded her intuition and avoided their predicament with this rough crowd. He hoped these guys were just uncouth, not dangerous.

As Jake declined the beer, Ray reached around the seat and groped Melinda. She leaped up out of the seat and yelled as if she'd accidentally sat down on a red-hot branding iron. That's just what Ray had expected her to sound like. He was having a good time now.

'Aww, come on guys,' Jake protested on Melinda's behalf. He was playing it down, trying to make them think he, too, was one of the guys.

Ray didn't take his protest well. His jaw clenched tightly, he turned on Jake. 'Got something to say?'

Behind the wheel, Bobby could detect the direction the conversation was going in the back seat. Without warning, he cut the wheel hard to the right. The truck careened, righted itself, and headed down a side dirt road off the beaten path. Melinda was getting panicky. 'Stop the truck,' she yelled to no avail.

'This is a short cut,' Bobby explained with a smirk that gave Melinda more cause for alarm.

'Short cut, nothing,' she screamed at him. 'Stop the truck!'

'Hey, guys,' Dillart called out, 'what do you think?' he continued, indicating Melinda suggestively.

Frightened, she cut him off. 'Listen guys, let's not . . .'

Again, Ray slipped his hand underneath Melinda and goosed her from behind. Jake started to open his mouth to complain, but Ray shot him a threatening look which made Jake think better of it. His hand straying to Melinda's halter top, Ray began to undo the bow that held it together in front.

Melinda's mouth was dry. She could barely manage to get the words out as Ray's fingers played with the string on her blouse. 'I don't like this, guys.'

'What are you both getting so testy about?' whined Dillart. 'This is a short cut. Jeez, what do you think we're going to do?'

The beer-drinking, rowdy trio laughed. They knew what they were going to do. And Melinda had good reason to be more than testy. While they laughed and slobbered all over their farm-boy plaid flannel shirts, Melinda's mind was racing, attempting to find a way to get out of this mess with the least amount of damage. Glancing at Jake, she could tell that even he was getting scared. It was time for her to take some kind of action, something which wouldn't trigger any violence but would get them safely out of there. She figured she didn't have much time. Bobby was getting excited. He leered at Melinda, getting ready for the fun he anticipated having with her.

Dillart put a reassuring hand on Melinda's knee; it was anything but reassuring. 'Don't get yourself in an uproar,' he told her. 'You're goin' to get where you're goin'.'

'And happier for the experience,' Ray added, his tone full of sexual innuendo. Then he turned to Jake, saying, 'And if you behave, we'll let you have some too.'

Jake sat paralysed with fear for his friend Melinda, as well as for himself. Melinda seemed to be taking it surprisingly calmly. Little did he know her emotional fabric was unravelling with each passing moment.

McCall prised open the storage shed – a small, coffin-like structure which was attached to the inside of the cabin. The warped door stuck at first, but a couple of goods pulls yanked it open to reveal a mouldy, dark interior. With a sweep of his hand, McCall brushed away the spider webs crisscrossing the shed. When the sunlight from outside penetrated, he could see broken pottery, axes, boards, gardening tools, rope, and assorted hardware. The oddest looking configuration was a cluster of small muskrat traps which dangled from the left wall; one of them, still opened, gaped like a tiny shark's mouth.

Pulling the axes out of the closet, McCall wiped the handles on the cuff of his shirt in a way which seemed altogether too civilized. It was hard for him to lose his sense of style, even in the sticks. His Equalizer persona never entirely disappeared, as Scott had too often complained. Having carefully cleaned the axe handle of dust and cobwebs, he picked up a second axe, but before he cleaned it, the open muskrat trap diverted his attention momentarily.

'Mukrat beware,' he said, musing aloud, and extended the axe handle to tap the muskrat trap several times; finally, its vicious little jaws snapped shut with a metallic clap. Amused, the Equalizer raised his eyebrows and regarded the effect of the trap on the axe handle with a kind of professional fascination. The thing clung to the handle like a crab. He detached it, as if it were a fish he'd caught, and tossed it back into the shed with the others.

An axe in hand, McCall shut the closet door and stepped outside the cabin. Walking around the side of the cabin, he found a pile of rough logs covered by a black plastic tarpaulin. Beside the pile were two large tree stumps which served as chopping blocks. He ripped the tarpaulin away, hefted a log off the pile, and prepared to chop wood for the fire. Wondering what his dad was doing, Scott came out of the front door. He was still changing clothes, putting on the new oversized LL Bean hunting shirt his father had given him.

Scott paused in the doorway as he heard his father split the first log. Absorbed in his own thoughts, he decided to take some time out from the household chores. He'd just finished cleaning the cabin; he wasn't ready to split logs. Sliding down onto the front porch, he sat, arms folded, as though we were observing some kind of truce. The dull thump of the axe blade striking wood punctuated the air. It was the only sound around. Funny, thought Scott, how in the city he just took noise for granted. Here in the woods it was almost disturbing not to have a constant hum in the background. All that noise was a reminder of his connection to the rest of humanity; at the moment, he felt very cut off from it.

Precise and expert at log splitting as he was at everything else he undertook, McCall cleanly split the piece of wood with two blows, then picked up another piece and set it on the block. Scott rose from the doorway and sauntered around the corner of the cabin where he stared silently at his father. Again, McCall raised the axe and brought it down, connecting with the wood. But, distracted by Scott's appearance, McCall struck a knot with the blade and the axe twisted at an awkward angle in his hand. Silently, and barely acknowledging Scott's presence, McCall repositioned the log on the stump. Taking the cue from his father, Scott picked up the second axe which leaned against the side of the cabin. McCall paused, wiping his brow. Scott took a thick log and, following his father's expert example, set it up on end and split it with two mighty heaves. Without pausing, he grabbed another, and another. McCall watched, pleased, then joined in again. As both of them fell into the steady rhythm of chopping wood and stacking it into a pile, they realized that, for the first time as father and son, they were working together towards a common goal. For a long while they didn't break the momentum, for fear the sense of common purpose and good feeling would fade away.

TWENTY

'Come on,' Dillart urged, prodding Melinda, squeezing her arm and stroking her hair.

'Stop it!' she protested. 'Let go of me.'

Bobby craned his neck around to get a glimpse of Dillart groping Melinda in the back seat. He had to admit he was envious. Why'd Dillart get to go first? Bobby owned the truck. It'd been his idea to pick her up. Oh, what the hell, he thought, he'd have his turn soon. But he didn't want to wait much longer. He'd found a good spot here along the river. Not many folks passed this way; besides, it would be getting dark soon and then they'd have all night . . .

Hitting the brakes, Bobby brought the pickup to an abrupt stop. The crowd in the back seat jerked forward. Ray spilled beer on Jake, whose willingness to abide the abuse was wearing thin. The fast-moving current and its rocky shore was a nagging reminder of how far they had come from civilization in the past hour. Any chance they had of being rescued by another car was gone. No one would find them now. He and Melinda were completely at the mercy of these creep country boys.

While Melinda continued to struggle against Dillart's grasp, he yanked her out of the cab, despite Jake's attempt to intercede. Jumping into the fray, Ray saw to it that Jake didn't mess with his buddy. 'Stay out of it, bub,' he told Jake, giving him a killer look.

Frustrated, Jake slumped back against the seat, crossed his arms and watched Dillart pulling Melinda roughly through the underbrush. Though it was hard to see clearly through the high reeds which bordered the river, Jake could discern a clearing which became more evident as Dillart and Melinda's footsteps trampled down some of the growth. Along the shore was a rotted, over-turned rowing boat. Taking this as great sport, Dillart forced Melinda onto the rowing boat, laughing uproariously and shooting grins back at his cohorts in the truck.

Melinda screamed, 'Take your hands off of me!' But the scream didn't do any good; it only caused him to grab her more tightly.

Back in the truck, Jake couldn't sit still any longer. No matter what the risk, he couldn't just let this goon rape Melinda. Ray and Bobby's attention was fixed on Melinda. Before they could notice, Jake had broken free of them and bolted towards the river. The two guys suddenly stopped laughing at Melinda's predicament and started running after Jake.

Melinda was pinned against the rowing boat. Holding her down, Dillart tugged at her blouse. It wasn't coming off as easily as he had imagined. Meanwhile Jake broke through the underbrush as fast as his legs could carry him. Ray and Bobby were right behind. Jake didn't have a chance. Jake felt a hand grabbing him from behind. The next thing he saw was Ray swinging him around. Ray cocked his arm back and let the punch fly directly into Jake's face. Jake fell backwards into a pile of sticks that had washed up along the river's banks. Ray and Bobby restrained him from getting back on his feet.

Triumphant, Dillart towered over Melinda. He began to

unbuckle his jeans. 'Now you're gonna give us something,' he told her. 'Make it easy.'

She had no intention of making it easy. Her arms flailed and her legs kicked at him as she struggled in vain against his greater physical strength. Repulsed by Dillart, Melinda spat on him. The next moment, Jake broke free of his captors.

'Run!' Jake shouted to Melinda.

Melinda turned to look at Jake who was charging Dillart like a mad ram. Jake ploughed into Dillart, catching him off guard and sending him sprawling across the rowing boat and onto the ground. While the two of them grappled in the soggy sand, Melinda made a break for it. She crashed through the underbrush. The brambles scratched her face as she ran along the shore and away from the truck in hopes of losing them in the foliage of the woods.

Once Jake saw that she had a good start, he left Dillart on the ground and ran after her. Ray and Bobby helped Dillart to his feet, then wasted no time in splitting up to catch Jake and Melinda.

Although they ran as hard as they could to escape, Melinda and Jake were no match for their more athletic pursuers. Bobby, Ray and Dillart closed in on them from both sides, forcing Melinda and Jake across a low lagoon. With nowhere to turn, they ran through the swampy marshes. Their shoes filled up with water, slowing them down. Their assailants gained on them. The noise of the couple sloshing through the water sent the ducks and birds scurrying up out of the surrounding reeds and into the air. The clamour of their squawking made Melinda more panicked. Then half way across the lagoon, Jake's foot sunk into the mud, causing him to lose his balance. He tripped and fell face forward into the shallow water. Already a few paces ahead of him, Melinda heard the splash, stopped, and went back for him.

No sooner had she turned around than she saw Ray and Bobby approaching, entering the water some twenty yards away. Frantic, Melinda gave Jake her hand and helped him up. Though he was dazed by the fall into the chilly water, he resumed his former pace and ran, making it with Melinda to the other side of the marsh where they disappeared behind the thick reeds.

Pausing for breath amid the reeds, Melinda and Jake tried not to breathe so loudly. But it was hard not to, fear and the expenditure of energy having made their bodies starved for air. Jake motioned for her to stay still.

Just when they thought they might have lost their pursuers, Dillart shattered the curtain of reeds. He was right on top of them now. Melinda didn't have a chance to escape. Before she knew what had hit her, Ray had her in his painful grip.

'Let go of me!' she shouted at the top of her lungs. 'Damn you, let go of me.'

The other bullies threw Jake to the ground. Bobby grabbed his legs as Ray shoved Melinda into Dillart's awaiting arms. Clutching her in an armlock, Dillart dragged her farther into the underbrush to finish what he'd started. He was determined to enjoy the sex with Melinda whether she did or not. The anticipation excited him.

Meanwhile, Ray rammed Jake, who was trying his best to get free of Bobby. Ray's fist caught him in the midriff, knocking the wind out of him; nevertheless, his adrenalin gave him the burst of energy he needed to wriggle out of Bobby's grasp. Bobby and Ray spun him around, and Ray connected with a punch to the neck that sent Jake reeling. Knocked to the ground, Jake, head first, struck a large, sharp rock.

In the reeds a short distance away, Dillart had Melinda pinned against the ground. Fending him off as long as she could, she felt the last of her strength ebb out of her. Dillart's brute force had won. She could continue to squirm, but she knew she'd lost the battle. Her eyes welled up with tears as Dillart's body pressed against hers, moving spasmodically up and down.

*   *   *

With their opponent lying unconscious on the ground, Bobby and Ray took a moment to catch their breath and check themselves for damage. They were both uninjured. But Jake wasn't. Bobby went over to Jake's still form and regarded him carefully.

'Hey,' he said, calling Ray over to see for himself. 'He ain't moving.'

Ray joined him and bent down beside Jake's body. He looked more closely for signs of life. There weren't any. Panic rising in his voice, he shouted in Dillart and Melinda's direction. 'Dillart, get over here.'

Dillart froze. Limp underneath him, her face streaked with tears, Melinda prayed for a reprieve. Maybe Dillart would heed his pals' call. Dillart considered it, then pressed against her harder.

Ray's shout was more urgent now. 'Dillart!'

This time Dillart caught the strain in Ray's voice. Knowing it must be something important, he stopped, pushed himself off Melinda, and crashed through the underbrush to see what had gone wrong.

Bobby and Ray were crouched by the body. Jake still lay motionless on the ground. The sight stopped Dillart dead in his tracks. Bobby was addressing Ray:

'Think you hurt him, Ray. Hurt him bad.'

Not wanting to believe it, Ray tapped Jake. 'Hey, bub, you all right?' Jake didn't respond. There was no sound, no movement. Ray's eyes began to dart wildly about as he was seized by the dread that he had killed a man. Bobby's accusatory tone didn't help matters much either.

'What'd you hit him so hard for?' Bobby asked.

'Hey,' Ray retorted, 'I barely touched him.'

Tying her blouse back together, Melinda staggered onto the scene in a daze. She gasped at the sight of her friend prostrate on the ground. 'Jake! Jake!'

The fury rising in her, she glared at Jake's assailants, then at Dillart. Suddenly Dillart was scared, too. Things had gone too far and gotten out of hand. They'd just wanted to have some fun. They hadn't meant harm. There was no way he could explain that to Melinda, or anyone else who would believe him. They'd better clear out while they could. The fun was over.

'Let's go, Bobby,' Dillart told him.

'Hey, I got my foot on the accelerator,' Bobby said, moving away from the spot as quickly as they could.

Free of her attackers at last, Melinda looked down at Jake's head and was horrified by the sight of his blood against the stone. Alone and abandoned in the marsh, she screamed. She was still screaming when she heard the distant roar of the pickup. Deserted, Melinda was completely alone and helpless – and certain that Jake was dead.

The noise of the truck's engine faded. If Jake weren't already dead, they'd guaranteed that he would be soon by abandoning him. Hysterical, Melinda didn't know where to turn. She sat down beside Jake and sobbed convulsively. Then she heard the sound of an engine again. Someone was coming. Her heart leapt with hope. Maybe they had a chance.

But as the engine drew nearer, her hopes were dashed. The three men reappeared in their truck, and from the serious expressions on their faces as they stepped towards her, she sensed they had murder on their minds.

While Melinda worried whether she was about to die, McCall and Scott continued on their marathon wood-chopping. The chore had developed into a kind of competition, with each of the men heaping the split logs into his own separate pile. No longer were they working towards the same goal, as it had seemed at first; they were pitted against one another, fuelled by Scott's determination to prove he was better than his father. Scott had youth on his side. Whereas his strokes were quick and powerful, McCall's were precise and smooth, conserving energy. The ease with which his father cut the wood ignited an irrational anger in Scott. The ever-increasing size of Scott's log pile – larger than his father's – gave Scott immense satisfaction. Scott was relentless, whacking at the wood viciously. His father flagged. Finally, he had to set his axe down and take a breather. The chopping had left him more winded than he thought.

'I'd better take some of this in,' he told Scott as he tried to get control of his breathing.

Scott took a deep breath and let loose with another blow at the wood. 'Yeah,' he said curtly. 'I'll keep chopping.'

Scott picked up the next log and went to work. Some holiday this was turning out to be, he thought, growing increasingly furious with his father. This certainly wasn't his idea of an intimate weekend outing to become reacquainted. He took out his anger on the wood until his father left, carrying a handful of split wood to the front of the cabin. When McCall was out of sight, Scott stopped chopping. Gingerly, he pulled his hand free of the axe handle. There was blood in his palm. His shoulders ached. He tried rolling them to relieve the hurt, but it didn't help much. Swallowing, he gripped the handle again and resumed chopping.

As McCall dropped the pile of wood by the hearth, he winced at the pain in his hand. He, too, had a bloody, broken blister to show for his labour. Of course, he could never admit to it; neither could Scott. As far as he knew, Scott wasn't feeling anything – and maybe that was the problem both of them shared most of all.

Driving down the winding roads which meandered through the backwoods near the cabin, the black pickup truck sped towards a small local hospital near the centre of King's Harbor. Numb with shock, Melinda sat in the back of the truck with Jake, who was still unconscious. The trip to the country clinic was a blur to her. The last thing she remembered was getting in the truck, and how grateful she was that they'd come back and hadn't killed her.

Some time later, a few minutes or maybe hours (Melinda couldn't tell), Melinda walked out from behind the white curtains surrounding Jake. Outside the hospital room, Bobby, Dillart and Ray tried to read the news on her face.

She looked right through them as she mumbled to herself, 'He's dead.'

TWENTY-ONE

Among the amenities in the cabin was a wood stove. That, an old refrigerator, and a few cabinets stocked with canned foods and spices, were the extent of the kitchen. It was a big, black, cast-iron affair with openings in the top to cook on, and a small oven inside its pot belly for baking. Another latched door under the oven opened for the kindling. The stove, or at least its prototype, had been named the Franklin stove, after its inventor Benjamin Franklin. From what Scott could tell of the stove's condition, Ben himself might have cooked on it.

McCall stoked the belly of the stove with kindling and lit the fire. In a few minutes, the stove would not only be primed for cooking a meal; it would have the room warmed to a nice, cosy temperature. The overhanging trees, the cabin's thick walls and its few windows tended to make the room cooler than the outdoors. Now that it was getting later in the day, they would need the stove's heat very soon.

Having had his share of chopping wood for the next

several years, Scott casually walked into the cabin. His dad was still bent over the stove. He appeared to be completely recovered from the rigours of wood splitting.

'We got any beer?' Scott asked him matter-of-factly. McCall realized he had forgotten to pick it up at the food co-op in town.

'No.'

'I'll run in and get some,' Scott offered and headed for the door. Before he stepped outside, he noticed his dad studying his bloody hand. 'Need anything else?'

McCall held up his hand, his prize for their contest, and gave Scott a wry smile. 'Some hydrogen peroxide for my hand.'

Scott smiled, holding up his own bloody hand for his father to see. 'I already had that covered. It was my first stop.'

Father and son looked at each other and their bloody hands and shared a heartfelt laugh that broke the tension and drew them closer together. Their blistered hands brought home to them the lengths they would go to prove themselves to each other, and to win each other's love; their hands, they realized simultaneously represented the beginning of a magnificent bonding between them.

Escorted by Bobby, Ray, and Dillart, Melinda emerged from the small clinic into the parking lot. The clinic, which was a prefabricated series of modular sections, had been erected in the late 1960s; a new wing was being added, expanding the hospital into the parking lot where Melinda was being led like a lost sheep by the three men. Dr Ness – a middle-aged, no-nonsense, native of Maine – watched through the reception area's glass doors. Something struck him as odd about the relationship between the girl and the three men, but he had no idea what it could be. He wondered if she was recovered enough from the emotional ordeal to be left unattended.

In the parking lot, Dillart was sternly giving her orders.

'You keep your mouth shut about this,' he told her. 'Understand?'

Melinda nodded vacantly.

'Now let it alone,' Ray joined in. 'Keep your mouth shut. We'll take you out of town.'

Suddenly Melinda began to lose the control she'd maintained since arriving at the hospital. She shrieked and sobbed simultaneously, and began to meander away from her three assailants, her face buried in her hands. Noticing her drastic change in behaviour, the doctor who had been observing her hurried out of the door and went to her side.

'Miss, are you sure you don't want to come back and lie down for a while?' he asked, taking her by the arm.

Ray stepped forward. His eyes shot Melinda a smouldering, threatening look.

'I'm all right,' she claimed, brushing the tears away. Dr Ness didn't seem convinced. But he couldn't make her stay against her will without good reason.

Ray took her by the arm, causing the doctor to loosen his grip. Dragging her across the parking lot, Ray yelled out to his buddies with false cheer, 'I need a beer.'

'I need a lot of beers,' Dillart echoed him.

The doctor, still concerned about Melinda, followed them to the pickup truck.

'Don't go too far,' Dr Ness cautioned them while he eyed them with suspicion. 'Sheriff Stone's going to want to see you. He's gonna want a complete report on how this happened.'

Bobby immediately became very defensive and said, sneering at the doctor, 'We ain't going anywhere.'

Just to lower the odds against their going, Dr Ness walked behind their black pickup and made a deliberate show of taking down the licence plate number.

A few minutes later, Ray, Bobby, and Dillart ushered Melinda into Ye Olde General Store, sat down at a table, and ordered a round of four beers. None of the locals in the café section of the store paid much attention to them. Even though folks routinely gathered here to eat, drink and exchange gossip, they pretended not to pay strangers any mind. At least till they left. *Then* they talked about them.

But it was considered rude to gossip about anybody unless you did it behind their backs.

The store and tavern had a rustic, comfortable, sloppy ambience. People still shovelled their flour and other staples out of big wooden barrels. Calendars of years gone by still hung on the wall. Old George, the butcher and short-order cook behind the counter, made up sandwiches to order. Holly Jay, the waitress, always wearing the same mini-skirt and bouffant hair-do, and always chewing gum, circulated to take drink and food orders from the patrons.

'You guys want anything besides boozeburgers?' Holly Jay smacked, flirting with Dillart.

Dillart grinned at her, then turned to Melinda. 'You hungry?' he asked her solicitously.

'Yeah,' piped up Bobby, 'get her a hamburger.'

'You want fries?' Holly Jay asked Melinda.

Bobby answered for her again, getting Holly Jay somewhat flustered and confused. 'Yeah. Get her fries.' Melinda, caught in the middle, didn't know what to say.

Holly Jay jotted down the order and went behind the counter. Rising suddenly from the table, Ray addressed his three companions. 'Come on, he said, nodding towards a less populated corner of the store. 'Let's talk.'

The three got up and moved away, leaving Melinda, alone and forlorn, at the table.

In the corner of the store, Dillart's face was bright red as he backed Ray up against the wall. 'What the hell did you hit him so hard for?'

'I didn't hit him hard,' Ray swore and stammered. 'I didn't . . .'

'Jesus!' exclaimed Bobby, challenging him. 'You killed him!'

'He died – but I didn't kill him.' Ray pleaded for their understanding, but he wasn't getting it; frustrated, he argued in his own defence. 'There's a difference. And I ain't in this alone. So don't try to drop this on my lap.'

Dillart clenched his jaw and spoke angrily through his teeth. 'So what're we gonna tell Stone?'

None of them had the answer to that question.

Melinda stared blankly out into space. People walked by her; they may as well not have been there. As Scott entered the store, she showed no sign of recognizing him. He stepped right up to the counter without glancing over towards the cluster of small tables by the pot-bellied stove. Holly Jay the waitress interrupted her scurrying around behind the counter to take his order.

'Can I have a cold one and two sixes to go?' Scott asked.

'Sure,' she said. She grabbed a cold beer from the case, and then went off to get a six pack.

Scott took a sip of the beer and turned to take in the surrounding room. It seemed bigger than it looked from the outside, and not so dilapidated either. The shelves were high, some going up to the rafters in the ceiling, and everything was neatly organized. There was a sign over the door that read: 'If you can't get it here, you probably don't need it.' He believed them. Scott's roving eye eventually fell on Melinda, who was still sitting alone at the table, and who appeared to be a lost, frightened child. Her trio of tormentors huddled in the corner by the window. Ray was trying to take control of the discussion. Keeping his distance, Scott regarded them suspiciously.

'We'll tell them he ran into a branch,' Ray suggested, making up yet another scenario which he hoped would sound closer to the truth than the last one. 'We were in the woods playing football . . . throwing frisbees . . . or . . .'

'A branch?' put in Dillart, not buying any part of Ray's far-fetched tale. 'He didn't have any marks on him.'

'He got whacked in the throat,' Bobby reminded them.

Ray hung his head in despair. Even the beer wasn't cheering him up. 'They'll never believe it.'

Dillart took on the role of group cheer-leader, his forced brightness a feeble attempt to buoy their spirits. 'If we hang together, why won't they believe it?' he asked.

His two friends thought about it, but lacked his swaggering confidence.

'What about her?' Bobby asked, nodding in Melinda's direction.

'She says she's going to Toronto,' said Dillart. 'Let's just take her to the interstate.'

Bobby was still worried. 'It doesn't matter where she is. It's what she says.'

'Oh, man, she's off her head,' Dillart said, trying to convince them that no one would believe her anyway. 'Look at her. Who knows what she's gonna say?'

Depressed, Melinda stared down at the table. She felt the presence of a man standing beside her, but she thought it was one of her captors. She was surprised to hear another voice.

'Hey, Toronto,' Scott greeted her. She looked up at him, not seeming to recognize his face at first. 'You didn't get too far.'

When she raised her head, he could see the tear stains and the red-rimmed eyes; even more obvious was the look of fear she couldn't shake, no matter how much crying she'd done.

'Hey, what's the matter?' Scott asked her.

Suddenly she blurted the words out. 'They killed Jake.' She nodded toward the three conspiring young men in the corner. 'And I think they're gonna kill me too.'

Dillart's voice boomed across the room at Scott. 'Get away from her.'

Scott looked at the source of the voice and saw Dillart, Ray and Bobby approaching him and Melinda. They looked anything by friendly. Their menacing expressions put Scott on his guard.

'Help me,' Melinda pleaded with him. The girl's helplessness was written in her face. Scott had to do something. But what?

Before he could grab Melinda and get her out of the store, Dillart was staring him in the face, challenging him. Scott pushed him away, which provoked Ray to swing at Scott. Managing to duck the punch, Scott drove his fist into Ray's stomach. Then Bobby's tall, tight body charged him. Scott picked up a chair and hurled it at him; the chair threw him off balance and sent him crashing into a table and onto the floor. Before the three could get back on their feet, Scott took Melinda's hand and the two of them raced out of the door.

133

The Jaguar was parked in front. Scott opened the passenger door and shoved Melinda inside. Fumbling for the key, he had it ready for the ignition by the time he jumped into the driver's seat. Out of the corner of his eye, Scott saw Ray bounding out of the door. Scott threw the Jag into gear and mashed the pedal all at once. Melinda screamed hysterically. The car shot forward. Ray threw himself at the back of the car, but it moved out too fast for him to get a footing. As the car jerked ahead, he slid off the trunk and hit the ground as the Jaguar screeched away.

Dillart and Bobby were right behind Ray. After helping their comrade to his feet, they made a dash for their pickup and took off in hot pursuit of the Jag. Meanwhile Scott and Melinda had a good head start on them. The car roared down the deserted Main Street. Scott wished there were someone around to see they were in trouble and call for help.

'Where's the police station?' he shouted at Melinda.

She shook her head. 'I don't know! I don't live here.'

'Look for a phone!'

Before Melinda could look, they had covered the short distance of Main Street and were entering the countryside. Not a sign of anyone anywhere – just hills, trees and brush. Scott had no idea where they were going. Much to Melinda's distress, he suddenly slammed on the brakes and went into a 180-degree skid. With the car facing the opposite direction now, Scott gunned the car and headed back towards the town.

Melinda was panicking, not knowing what Scott had in mind. Maybe he was going to turn her over to the three cretins again. 'What are you doing?' she asked frantically, her tone pleading. 'No!'

'My Dad'll know what to do!'

The Jag sped towards Main Street. The truck, coming from the opposite direction in sluggish pursuit, charged straight at them. Scott braced his nerves. If they wanted to play chicken with him, he'd play along, but he wouldn't let them intimidate him. Scott and Melinda held their breath.

Just when the pickup seemed to be on top of them, the truck slammed on the brakes and skidded out to the side of the road. Scott swerved, passing the truck and barrelling away. From what he could discern in his rear-view mirror, the truck was disabled. Now if it would only stay out of commission long enough for him and Melinda to make it safely back to the cabin . . .

TWENTY-TWO

Melinda was beginning to calm down. Scott's dare-devil driving had led her to believe for a moment that she had traded in one set of lunatics for another. But his genuine concern for her welfare and his level-headedness became apparent as he wound through the backroads to the cabin he was sharing with his father for the weekend. There was a sensitivity and maturity about Scott that made Melinda trust him. She was even beginning to feel safe.

The cabin was as secluded and as rustic as Scott had described it to her. But Melinda didn't care what it looked like by the time Scott pulled the Jaguar up to the clearing in front and parked it. She was just happy to have found a refuge, a retreat where she could put back the pieces before deciding what the next step was in her life.

Lucky for Melinda's peace of mind, she and Scott couldn't see that the boys in the pickup had followed them to the cabin. The damage to their truck looked worse than it was, and they'd had no trouble starting it and resuming the chase where they'd left off. In a town as small as King's

Harbor, it wasn't hard to follow a car, especially if you knew the back roads, and if the car stood out as much as a black Jaguar did. The car's tracks on the dirt roads were a dead giveaway. Dillart, Ray and Bobby were right behind them, hanging back only far enough so that Scott and Melinda wouldn't know it.

Bobby brought the truck to a quiet, secluded spot not far from the cabin. Hidden by trees and brush, they could observe everything without being seen. They slipped out of the truck and crouched to spy Scott taking Melinda into the cabin and introducting her to an older, grey-haired man.

'Now what?' Bobby asked his two friends.

'I didn't know anybody was using this place,' Ray said, wondering who the kid and the older man could be; certainly not any folks from around here.

'Where are those plates from?' asked Dillart.

Ray peered closely through the trees. 'New York,' he answered.

Inside the cabin, McCall finished listening to the story of Melinda's ordeal, or at least enough of it to realize the urgency of the situation. Experience told him that the killers wouldn't stop until they'd tracked Melinda down, too. It was a small town. They were bound to find her sooner or later. The cabin had an old, black desk phone. McCall reached for it and picked up the receiver.

'We have to call the authorities!' he told Scott and Melinda. As he put the phone to his ear, his face dropped. Scott could see something was wrong. 'It's dead.'

Earlier in the day McCall had checked the phone and it was working fine. He suspected the line had not gone dead on its own accord. Getting up, he walked over to the window and looked outside. On the telephone pole a short distance away was a young man who worked his way down the pole. He wore sneakers, jeans and a dirty T-shirt, and didn't look like a company lineman. From what Melinda had told him, the man on the telephone pole was the same who had raped her: Dillart. At the bottom of the pole, two other young farm boys, one tall and lean, the other

137

pudgier, waited for their buddy to climb down. At the top of the pole, McCall noticed, was a bundle of slashed wires which explained why the phone was suddenly dead.

Dillart finished climbing down the pole. His hands were grimy. He wiped them off on his jeans and checked for splinters.

'We got to find out who's inside and what they got,' Dillart told his cohorts.

Bobby didn't like the way things were going. The nervousness and hesitation were evident in his voice. 'What are we getting into?' he asked the other two.

'We're not *getting* into anything,' Ray informed him sarcastically. 'We're already there.'

Bobby nodded his understanding. Whether he wanted any part of this or not, he had to play along with his pals. Dillart and Ray always came up with better ideas than he did anyway.

'But we're talking about killing the girl, the kid, and whoever else is in that cabin,' Dillart explained, acting the role of devil's advocate.

Plainly scared and desperate, Ray wheeled around and argued: 'We're talking about *us* – turning into old men in a four by eight prison cell! No more chicks. No more beers. No more fishing. No more life. No more nothing. Now I'll tell you what.'

The bleak picture of the future had a sobering effect on Bobby and Dillart. Ray slid through the brush and grabbed a rifle from inside the cab of the truck. Dillart and Ray watched with curiosity as he returned with the gun and shoved it into Dillart's hands. Ray was near tears.

'You shoot me or you shoot them,' he told Dillart. 'Because if one of them lives to tell what we did, I don't wanna live. I mean it, Dil. I've known you and Bobby all my life, and I value you more than . . . more than them.'

Bobby stared silently at Dillart, reading him, then said, 'That goes for me too, Dil.'

Dillart guessed there was no other choice. He sighed, resigned to the violent course of action. 'All right,' he agreed.

'Now here's what we do,' Ray told him, taking charge. 'I'm gonna take the truck back in. You fire once into the front of the cabin soon as I'm gone, so they know you're out here. Then you run like a damn rabbit round the back and fire another shot. Then stay covered. Keep watching. I'll be back.'

Bobby, distressed and doubtful they could make the plan work, shook his head. 'Man, I don't like this.'

'Suck it up,' Dillart told him. 'We got to hold this together.'

Dillart's advice didn't keep Bobby from being overcome by a wave of nausea. He felt as if his whole life were slipping away from him. Earlier they'd all been having such a good time, riding around, drinking beer; now they were talking about killing people. He'd hunted deer lots of times. That was different. He imagined shooting the occupants of the cabin. A picture of bloody carnage came to his mind. Then there was always the nagging question: What if they got him before he got them?

Dillart could tell Bobby was letting his fears get the best of him. He punched him hard on the shoulder, jarring Bobby back to reality and getting his attention. Meanwhile, Ray jumped into the driver's seat of the cab, revved the engine, and drove off down the dirt road.

Inside the cabin, McCall assumed his role of the Equalizer as he prepared for the worst – an onslaught by the animals who had ravaged Melinda and killed her boyfriend. He threw the rusty door bolt into place. Taking the old rocking chair, he removed the pillow and handed it to Melinda, then jammed the chair up against the door, just in case the bolt didn't hold. Scott cocked his ear against the shuttered window to detect any alarming sounds. He could make out the roar of the truck as it took off down the road.

'That's their truck moving out,' he told his father. 'Think maybe they're going?'

'No,' said McCall, certain they weren't going. He suspected the truck's departure was just a trick to lull Melinda and the McCalls into a false sense of security.

The next sound they heard was a bullet smashing through the glass.

As the bullet shattered the glass, then came through the shutter, Scott jerked back, barely avoiding it. He crouched instinctively. Seized with terror again, Melinda looked apprehensively at the Equalizer. Scott wondered what his father's next move would be. The bullet didn't seem to faze him at all; he remained perfectly cool and calm.

'Come on,' he told Scott and Melinda matter-of-factly, 'we have work to do.'

TWENTY-THREE

The sun went down. It went down in a pink and orange array of streaks across the partially cloudy sky. It went down, and McCall, Scott, and Melinda saw only the streaks of light fade through the cracks and the bullet hole in the shutters. Darkness had come outside. The real danger would soon begin.

Inside, the fire in the Franklin stove cast shadows against the walls while providing a flickering orange glow that lit the room. The only other light came from a single bare bulb hanging from a cord in the middle of the room. A pile was stacked under the light bulb. McCall, Scott, and Melinda had been gathering things since the shot rang out. The heap consisted of odds and ends combed from drawers, closets, and cabinets in the cabin; things which might prove useful when the attack came. They were sure it would come. They weren't sure when.

Melinda approached the pile with a group of objects she'd rounded up about the cabin. In her hands were a fishing tackle box, flyrods, hooks – virtually everything you'd need for a fishing trip. McCall had asked her to gather anything that might help. Though she wasn't sure what good this odd assortment of objects might be, she offered them as her contribution to the pile.

'Will these help?' she asked the Equalizer.

'Are there any hooks inside?'

Melinda set the tackle box down atop a small table, and pulled out a large, gnarly fishing hook.

'Yeah, there's a bunch of them.'

'Empty it on the pile,' McCall instructed her.

Meanwhile Scott emerged through the door of the storage closet which jutted out beyond the interior wall of the cabin and sunk a few feet below the level of the cabin floor. Stepping up the two steps into the cabin, Scott carried with him the collection of muskrat traps, three car flares, a box of nails, and a box of wooden kitchen matches.

'Matches,' Scott said, holding them up proudly. 'Hope they're not too damp.'

They looked okay to the Equalizer; besides, they had the fire in the stove if they needed it. Suddenly McCall noticed Melinda straying over near the shutters.

'Melinda! Stay away from those windows!' Heeding his warning, she immediately jumped back and ran over to Scott. The Equalizer studied the collection of objects in the middle of the room, then turned to Scott and Melinda. 'Keep gathering. We need more things: rope, nails, anything that'll burn. Move. Both of you,' he instructed them, then added, 'And keep alert. We don't know how they'll attack. Or when.'

Melinda followed Scott as he went over to the bed and got down on the floor to search under them.

'I'm scared,' she told Scott, and crouched down on the floor beside him.

He laughed. 'I have a feeling it goes with the territory.'

Somewhat relieved by Scott's sense of humour about the situation, Melinda got up and began checking out the cabinets near the stove. The pine cabinets contained mostly food items, but she managed to find a small can of sterno hidden among the canned vegetables. McCall was appraising the usefulness of the objects in the pile when Melinda offered him the sterno.

'I know this will burn,' she told him uncertainly, 'but I don't know if it's what you need.'

The Equalizer took the can, then looked at Melinda.

'By itself it will do little,' he told her, ruminating about ways the sterno could be put to use. 'But . . . yes, thank you.'

'I flunked chemistry,' Melinda said apologetically. 'Twice.'

McCall smiled, and resumed his rummaging through the contents of the pile.

A bright moon lit the woods surrounding the cabin. Their eyes adjusted to the darkness. Dillart and Bobby could see well enough to move around without tripping over any unseen obstacles which lay between them and the cabin. Their first strategic target was the Jaguar that sat parked not far from the cabin door. Crawling along the ground to lessen the chances of his being seen, Dillart inched his way towards the car. The hunting knife in its sheath dragged along the ground with him. When he reached the car, Dillart and Bobby, who was close behind him, hid behind the car's front end. Bobby moved to the rear of the car while Dillart unsheathed the hunting knife. Slowly pressing its point into the side of the front tyre, he watched and listened as the air hissed out. In a matter of seconds, the tyre was on its way to becoming flat; that done, he scooted along the side of the car to Bobby.

'I spotted the fuse box by the side,' Bobby told him, pointing out the small wooden box which jutted out from the cabin.

'Take it out,' Dillart ordered. Bobby nodded, and darted toward the side of the cabin. Dillart pulled out his knife and smiled, satisfied, as the back tyre went flat.

Inside the cabin, the Equalizer kept a wary eye on the front windows as he examined the items they'd gathered.

They didn't seem to have left anything out. The collection was an impressive one, considering it was put together on such short notice. It included Mason jars, paint thinner, powders in boxes and cans, a large block of paraffin wax, old rifle shells, book matches, some kids' games, Chinese checkers, spoons, table knives, a small rusty scythe, and gardening tools.

Along the outside of the cabin, Bobby opened the fuse-box and pulled out the circuit breaker. Suddenly the single light bulb inside went out. Now there was only the constant flame in the stove to light the room.

'I expected that,' McCall told Melinda and Scott, barely reacting to the power cut off. 'I need wire. Zipcord. Get it anywhere,' he instructed them, pointing to the wall. 'Rip it off the panelling, the light fixtures, telephone.' As Melinda jumped at his orders, he grabbed her and handed her the block of wax. 'Find a pan,' the Equalizer added to the list of instructions. 'Melt the wax down.'

Then they suddenly grew still. There was a new, ominous sound outside. Scott edged his way cautiously to the window and peered through the crack in the shutters.

The pickup truck was returning. It pulled up in front of the cabin. Ray jumped out, and his two pals soon joined him. From what little Bobby could see in the moonlight, Ray had brought three rifles, plus a couple of packs of beer and bottled booze with him. Apparently, they were going to dig in for the siege. Nervous, Bobby popped the top of a beer can.

'Maybe we should talk to them,' he suggested to the other two.

Ray scoffed at the idea. 'What are we gonna say?' he asked Bobby, who – lost for an answer – shrugged his shoulders.

Bobby took a swig of beer and thought about the possible repercussions of their actions. 'I don't like what we're doing, Dil.'

His moral qualms sent Ray into a flying rage. Before Bobby knew what had hit him, Ray was flinging him up against the truck. Bobby felt the hard metal jab into his spine.

'You don't like it,' Ray shouted out of control. 'You don't like it!'

Playing the brains of the outfit, as well as the peacemaker, Dillart stepped in, grabbing Ray by the arm. 'Back off, Ray. We've got to stick together on this.' Then he locked glances with Bobby, seeking his commitment. 'Right, Bobby?'

Still uncertain, Bobby nodded anyway.

'Okay, okay,' grumbled Ray, backing off of Bobby. 'Get me a beer, will ya?'

Melinda dropped the paraffin into a black cast iron skillet and began melting it as the Equalizer had instructed. The sound of voices outside didn't escape McCall, but it didn't bother him either. Like a trained chemist, he went about the job of scientifically blending the various liquids and powders in the Mason jars. Hovering anxiously by the window, Scott looked to his father for some kind of reassurance. Scott's own edginess only served to make Melinda all that much more jumpy. Knowing they couldn't perform their tasks well if their nerves were shattered, the Equalizer tried to allay their fears.

'For a while they're going to do nothing,' McCall told them. 'As scared as you are, that's how scared they are. Luckily, they're amateurs. A professional would walk through that door right now and that would be the end of us.'

'What if they do that?' Scott asked, his voice getting higher and cracking under pressure. 'What if they do come in right now?'

'Then I was wrong,' McCall said, smiling, then moved over to the table and arranged the Mason jars in neat rows, as if they were on an assembly line. McCall pointed to the wire along the baseboard. Taking the cue, Scott went back to yanking it out.' 'We'll need the longest lengths you can find, Scott. Strip both ends.' Then he turned to Melinda,

145

who was still stirring the wax over the stove, and asked, 'Any foil in the kitchen?' She went back to the kitchen cabinets and was searching when she heard him add: 'Chewing gum?'

She hadn't seen any gum in the cabinets. But she thought she might have some on her. Patting the pockets of her jeans, Melinda came up with a twisted pack. On closer inspection, she found it contained only two sad-looking sticks. She wondered if they'd be enough to do any good and threw them down on the table.

The Equalizer busied himself with his eight Mason jars lined up on the table. He carefully measured paint thinner, turpentine, and assorted liquids and powders. Meanwhile Scott was occupied at the window, stripping the ends of the telephone wire according to his father's instructions. He assumed they were making some sort of firebomb, but he wasn't sure how it would work or what it would do – or even *if* it would work. But he did know that if it didn't work, they'd all be sitting ducks when the assault came.

'Scott!' McCall called across the room. 'How's it going out there?'

Cautiously, Scott peeked through the shutters again. 'Nothing moving,' he reported, then showed his father the wire. 'How's this?'

McCall glanced at the stripped ends. 'Fine.' Melinda stood behind him, poised over his assembly line of Mason jars. 'Tear the gum wrappers into eight equal parts,' he ordered Melinda. 'About this size,' he said, indicating with two raised fingers. 'Is the wax ready?'

Melinda moved over to the stove and checked the pan. 'Yes,' she reported. She set the gum aside.

'No, no,' McCall told her, glancing her way as he continued working on the Mason jars. 'Save the gum. We'll need it for later.'

Scott resumed his vigil at the window. Although it was difficult to discern much in the dark, he thought he saw shadows moving, or maybe it was just his mind playing tricks. Pressed against the wall, he noticed something above

146

his head he'd somehow missed in their search of the cabin. Mounted on the wall were two antique flintlock duelling pistols. 'All right,' he said to himself at the sight of them. He reached for the pistols and took them down to show his father his lucky find. 'Dad, check this out.'

'What's that?' McCall said, looking up at the pistols as Scott extended them towards him. McCall's eyes widened at the sight of them. 'Good work, Scott.'

'Maybe there are bullets some place for them,' Scott said, glancing around.

McCall was amused by his son's ignorance of antique guns. 'Flintlocks don't use bullets,' he explained. 'They work with ball and cap.' Taking the guns, McCall set them aside. 'I'll take care of those in a minute.' He resumed his work on the Mason jars. 'Let's finish this first,' he told Scott and Melinda, and handed them each gum, then ordered: 'Chew.'

Silly as it seemed at a time such as this, they popped the gum in their mouths and began chewing. If nothing else, the gum relieved some of their nervous tension.

The black pickup truck had become the fortress for the three young men as they prepared to storm the cabin. So far they'd armed themselves, cut off their hostages' access to telephoning the outside world, removed their electrical power, and prevented them from escaping by slashing their tyres. They were proud of themselves, and heady with power, their headiness magnified by all the alcohol they'd consumed. The drinking made it easier. It helped them keep their wits about them, or so they thought, as they deluded themselves with one beer after another.

Hunched behind the truck, they began to map out their strategy.

Ray took a swig of his beer and asked Dillart, 'How do you think we should play this?'

'Maybe we can talk to them,' Bobby suggested again.

'Sure, Bobby,' said Ray, disgusted with Bobby's refrain that they talk to their captives. 'Invite them over for a beer,' he said facetiously.

Bobby cowered as Dillart laughed at Ray's sarcasm. 'We got the rifles and ammo enough to make toothpicks of that cabin,' Dillart told his comrades-in-arms.

'If anything moves, waste it,' said Ray with false bravado.

Dillart took up a shotgun and pointed it squarely in Bobby's scared face. 'Fetch me a brew, boy,' he ordered him boldly. 'I got work to do.'

Happy to see he had an ally in Dillart, Ray snickered at Bobby. Now it was two against one.

Bobby pleaded with Dillart. 'I just think we should think this over, Dil. We're talking murder.'

'We're already talkin' murder,' Ray came back at him.

'Our word against theirs,' Bobby retorted.

'And I aim to see that their word is never heard,' Dillart growled at Bobby, ordering him about like a lackey. 'Now get me that brew.'

Ray and Dillart scoffed at the way Bobby, obviously intimidated, scrambled to get Dillart the beer. Grabbing the beer from Bobby, Dillart gave him a contemptuous smirk, then ventured out from behind the truck and moved quietly towards the cabin.

TWENTY-FOUR

Constructing weapons from household materials was nothing new to McCall. It was covered in the basic survival course when he entered the Agency. Over the years, he'd had to make weapons from scratch during only the rarest of dire circumstances; fortunately, he hadn't lost his touch where assembling your basic concussion grenade was concerned. The procedure was quite simple, actually, once you had the proper materials. He sealed the Mason jars, put the gum wrapper caps into the top, sealed them with chewing gum, and ran the phone wire off the caps.

Scott and Melinda were fascinated and astounded by the speed and agility with which he assembled the grenades. Although Scott had fantasized about his father's covert line of work before, he'd never had any concrete evidence till now. Though there were no doubt less stressful ways for his father to share his life as an intelligence operative, Scott felt privileged to be not only a witness to McCall's work, but a participant. The life-and-death situation of the moment would be something neither would ever forget. Already

Scott was less critical of his father's sophisticated skills and the uses to which he put them.

'We're going to have to place two of these on each side of the house,' the Equalizer explained to Scott and Melinda.

The idea of doing anything that risky astounded Melinda. 'How're we gonna do that?' she asked naively.

'There's a two foot crawl space beneath us,' McCall told them.

'How do you know that?' asked Scott. McCall fixed his son with a meaningful stare; suddenly Scott smiled, remembering what his father had told him about the 'spy' he'd sheltered here some time ago. 'Sorry,' Scott apologized. 'I forgot you've been here before.' Then he brightened to the thought of giving his dad a hand in this new, risky aspect of the operation. Scott solemnly told his father: 'I'll do it.'

McCall nodded, silently proud of Scott for taking the challenge. Scott watched as his father moved towards the back of the room and scrutinized the floorboards. Finally he stopped at a certain section, bent over to look at it more closely, and tested it with his foot. 'Here,' he called, motioning to Scott.

As Scott prised open the trap door in the floor inside the cabin, Dillart crept through the yard, closer to the side of the house. With a single Mason jar concussion grenade in his hand, Scott inched his way through the clods of dirt and rock under the cabin floor. Hearing a rustling noise – the sound of Dillart's feet – he paused and held his breath. Dillart rounded the back side of the cabin, his feet passing within two feet of Scott's face. Scott waited until they had passed, then slid one of the Mason jars into place by the rear corner of the cabin. Then he withdrew, working his way back to the trap door to get another bottle. His father handed him the jar. Taking the jar with one hand, Scott pointed with the other to the opposite side of the cabin where Dillart had moved. McCall nodded his understanding. With another concussion grenade in hand, Scott prepared to slip back under the house.

The Equalizer, carrying a chair with him, quickly took up a position by the side window. On guard by the shutters, he waited for Dillart to make his move. A shadow passed by outside as Dillart, pressed against the pane, tried to see in. From inside, the Equalizer waited for the right moment, then heaved the chair at the window. The window erupted in a shower of glass; Dillart, caught in its path, retreated, his face stinging with minor cuts.

Seeing his father's success with the chair trick, Scott took off through the trap door again. Under the boards of the cabin, he could hear the thump of Dillart's footsteps beating a fast path back to his buddies at the truck. Then he caught the sound of Bobby's worried voice:

'What happened. We heard . . . ?'

'I didn't even get a shot off,' Dillart complained, the wind taken somewhat out of his sails. He was too embarrassed to explain about the glass.

Ray reached out and grabbed the Ruger rifle. 'Well, I'll get a shot off.' Ray searched the ground for something, then picked up a large rock which he tossed to Bobby. Taken by surprise, Bobby fumbled the rock, nearly dropping it. Ray pointed at the cabin and gave Bobby new orders: 'When I get to that corner, take out that window there.'

Bobby couldn't believe his ears. Had Ray gone completely crazy? 'What are you gonna do?' he asked him.

'I'm goin' in,' Ray said, sneering. He puffed his chest out, flaunting his drunk, macho bravado. 'This is it! All or nothing.'

Inside the cabin, McCall's eye fell on a pair of interesting unglimpsed objects – a baby carriage and a teddy bear. Indicating them to Melinda, he said, 'Bring that over here.' She glanced at the carriage and stuffed animal and wondered what in the world he could possibly want them for. By now, Melinda had the sense that he knew what he was doing, and wouldn't bother him with questions. She trusted the Equalizer completely. Moments later, he was removing the wheel from the baby carriage.

Meanwhile, Ray approached the corner of the cabin and looked back at Bobby and Dillart. Clutching the rock, Bobby nervously awaited his signal.

'Throw the rock, Bobby,' Ray yelled.

Bobby hesitated. Dillart had no qualms about storming the cabin. He grabbed the rock from Bobby and heaved it toward the window.

Just as McCall had removed the wheel, the rock crashed through the window. The noise and the splintering glass stunned Melinda. She screamed, McCall grabbed her and pulled her down, covering her body with his.

Ray popped up into the open window, shoved the gun barrel inside the cabin and, without bothering to take aim, sprayed the room with bullets. The barrage lasted only a matter of seconds. His bravado spent, he yanked the gun from the window and bolted for the safety of the truck.

Scott hurriedly crawled under the cabin and clambered back inside the room through the trap door. 'You okay?' he asked his father and Melinda in the aftermath of the gunfire.

Both the Equalizer and Melinda were unharmed. 'You set?' McCall asked his son.

'They're all in place,' Scott told him, and thought he glimpsed a brief smile of pride on his father's face.

Running hunched over, Ray scurried behind the protective shield of the truck.

'I think I got one of them,' he said boastfully, lying to Bobby and Dillart.

Bobby seemed on the brink of tears. 'You sure?'

'Of course I'm sure,' Ray shot back, letting Bobby know there was no reason to discuss the matter further.

Ray's tough talk excited Dillart and got his adrenalin flowing. Excited and wild-eyed, he snatched the rifle from Ray's hands.

'I take out the next one,' Dillart told them both. Then Dillart shot a condescending look at Bobby, and, putting him down, remarked, 'And you, Bobby, can have the last one.' Grinning, Dillart reached for another beer to fortify him. He chugged the brew in pure macho fashion, wiping the liquid from the corners of his mouth. As an after-thought, he turned to Bobby and said, 'You can have the girl, too – if you think you can handle it.'

Giving Bobby a twisted grin, Dillart moved away from the truck and made his way towards the cabin. The gun was slung casually at his side. Watching the house from behind a group of nearby rocks, Dillart followed the shadow of a moving figure at the window. He poked his head over the top of the rocks, took aim, and fired.

The bullet blew apart another pane of glass at one of the windows. A few pieces of the glass shards scraped Melinda, who had been crouched not far from the window.

'Down. I said stay down,' shouted McCall at Melinda. 'Both of you.'

Scott scooted over to Melinda and gently touched her shoulder. 'Are you okay?'

She felt the sting from one cut on her hand. She shrugged it off as if it were nothing. 'It's not too bad,' she told him. Scott took a closer look. It looked pretty bad to him.

'I think it's about time we gave those boys a lesson in fair play,' McCall told Melinda and Scott. They couldn't have agreed more. Smiling at each other, they had the strong feeling that the tide was about to turn.

TWENTY-FIVE

Dillart was drinking the hard stuff now. Whisky. It went down like fire. It was like gasoline inflaming his frustration.

'What'd you get?' Ray asked him.

Dillart didn't feel like talking. He took another swig. 'Nothing,' he grumbled back at Ray. 'Glass.'

Ray eyed Dillart quizzically, but could tell from the annoyance in his voice that he ought to hold off on the questions for a while.

Having demonstrated his own method of building concussion grenades, the Equalizer set about the business of teaching Scott and Melinda to assemble flintlocks; actually, it was more a matter of reconditioning the antique firearms and manufacturing the ammunition.

McCall placed an old rifle shell on the table. Taking a jacknife, he split open the shell and spilled the dark gun powder on top of a yellowed newspaper. Nearby Melinda took the teddy bear and followed McCall's instructions. Her sentimentality holding her back, she was hesitant to split open the bear, but finally she ripped the stuffed animal open, extracting some of the wadding from inside. The Equalizer shifted his attention to the baby carriage. Taking the ball bearings from the wheel of the carriage, took a handful of them, and placed them on the table. They joined the powder and the wadding as he shoved them into the mouths of the flintlocks.

The guns were loaded and ready. Admiring his handiwork, he laid them out on the newspapers atop the table. Melinda and Scott looked on in amazement.

'The only question is whether they'll kill the person in front or behind them,' McCall said with grim humour. Scott laughed at his father's black humour. Melinda didn't.

While the McCall clan prepared their arsenal inside the cabin, the rural marauders huddled together by the truck and gave some thought to a change of tactics. They were helped along in their thinking by a change of libation, Dillart and Ray having swapped the whisky for a small bottle of blackberry brandy. Bobby showed little interest in their drinking or their plotting.

'This ain't gonna get it,' Dillart complained, taking another hit off the bottle. 'We can be pot-shotting them for a week and hitting nothing.'

'Yeah, so what do you suggest?' asked Ray, who was every bit as fed up with the situation as his comrade. He was ready to throw caution to the wind. 'We rush the place?'

Dillart contemplated, took another swig, and contemplated some more. 'At least get close enough to get a shot.'

Ray was willing to go along with that, or just about anything at that point. Hell, he would have just about jumped off a cliff if Dillart had asked him to in his present condition. Bobby wasn't so drunk, or so willing to go along; so he would hang back and provide cover. Dillart, who talked a big game, hung back with him while Ray advanced with the rifle.

The calm outside was beginning to arouse McCall's suspicions as he finished rigging the switches for the grenades. Working at a rapid pace, McCall loaded six wires to a board which he had jerry-rigged to trip of the Mason jar explosives. Then he removed the D-cell battery from the flashlight, attached a wire from the plant, and screwed it on top. The battery gave him cause for concern.

'Let's hope it has some juice left,' he told Scott and Melinda. Scott remembered how weak the battery had been when they arrived. Stationed at the window, he took another look outside.

'They're not here,' Scott told his father. 'I don't see them anywhere.'

'Check the other side,' McCall ordered him. 'Quick.'

Keeping below window level, Scott scurried across to the other side of the cabin. As his head came up, Dillart opened fire from outside. In the explosion and flash from the gun which followed, McCall saw Scott fall to the floor. He appeared to be uninjured.

'Get down!' McCall shouted.

A few feet from the window, Ray cocked his carbine. Just then, the Equalizer picked up one of the wires on the jerry-rigged board and touched it to a nail. Ray was about to rise up and jam the barrel of the gun when the first grenade went off.

The explosion shook the earth and the foundations of the cabin, lit up the outside with its blast, and sent Ray reeling. The gun clattered to the ground amid the flying debris. As the impact of the blast struck, Dillart dashed from the truck and pulled Ray back from the cabin. Ray was stunned but conscious.

'The rifle,' Ray shouted to Dillart. 'Get the rifle.'

Bobby charged by them, bending over, and scooped the rifle off the ground where Ray had dropped it. McCall caught sight of him retrieving the rifle. Before Bobby could retreat to the safety of the truck, McCall set off a second grenade, which knocked Bobby off his feet.

Inside the cabin, McCall saw the flash of the explosion and felt the impact, as did Melinda and Scott. McCall turned to the two of them for their reaction, Melinda smiled, and gave him the thumbs up sign. Impressed with his father's combat abilities, Scott cheered wildly.

'Way to go, Pop,' he yelled, causing his father to regard him oddly and wince.

'Scott, I know we've had our differences,' McCall told his son. 'But I must insist that you never again – under any circumstances or for any reason whatsoever – call me "pop".' Scott looked at his father sheepishly. 'Make that part of the truce. Agreed?'

'Agreed,' Scott said, nodding.

Having recovered from the blast of the second grenade, Bobby crawled back to the truck with the rifle. His impulse act of derring-do had given him renewed esteem in Ray and Dillart's eyes. The three quickly regrouped, devised a new plan of attack, then split up into different directions.

Ray took the front window. In the brief lull after the grenade blast, he crept to just under the sill. Catching his victims by surprise, he jumped up and, with the barrel of his rifle, swept the window clear of glass. As he'd seen in many of his favourite Clint Eastwood Westerns, Ray began blasting away inside the cabin without bothering to aim.

Melinda screamed as she saw the fire spitting through the windows. The bullets ploughed randomly into the cabin, shattering glass, splintering the wood, knocking objects from tables. The roar was deafening. Melinda thought a cannon had opened fire. Hysteria had her in its grip. For her protection, the Equalizer instinctively threw himself at her, diving on top of Melinda and knocking her to the floor. Scott, who was desperate to retaliate in some way, grabbed the flintlocks. Meanwhile, the rifle continued to fire away.

Outside Bobby and Dillart fanned out into positions, one taking the front entrance, the other taking the back. Scott sensed their movements. His priority had to be to stop the steady gunfire. Pressing himself against the cabin's interior wall, he slid along it, staying clear of the muzzle of the gun. With one hand, he grabbed the gun barrel; with the other, he pointed the flintlocks at Ray, ducked his head, and fired.

Ray felt the tug on his rifle before he saw the explosion.

157

For a moment, he thought his gun had backfired. It may as well have; for when Scott pulled the trigger on the flintlock pistols, the whole flintlock exploded in Ray's face. The flash alone blinded him temporarily. He fell backwards, releasing the rifle, which Scott yanked into the cabin.

Once Scott had the rifle in his possession, he turned it around and began emptying it over Ray's head, into the trees. The bullets split branches and blew leaves everywhere. Scott was like a mad one-man Army unleashed on their attackers.

'I'll kill you!' he shouted out into the night, challenging the three. 'Come on, you bastards.'

His voice struck terror into Dillart and Bobby. They both thought better of trying to crash the doors to the cabin; instead, they ran for cover. Dillart scrambled for safety behind a tree. Bobby rolled behind a pile of rocks. The firestorm continued around them. Ray pulled himself off the ground. He felt the blood running down his smudged face. The powder burn from the flintlocks spread a searing pain through his skin. Still unable to see, he stumbled blindly towards the woods.

'Scott!' McCall shouted. Thinking Scott had lost control and was taking unnecessary risks, McCall jumped up and pulled his son to the floor.

Enraged and angry, Scott pulled away from him. This was his fight now. He was old enough to take care of himself. But before that, he was going to prove to his father that he wasn't afraid of anything, including a band of mindless killers.

TWENTY-SIX

A blue haze of smoke, the residual from the gunpowder, hung inside the cabin. McCall, Scott, and Melinda could still smell the pungent odour of sulphur. Even in the darkness they could make out the wreckage. Glass glistened on the cabin floor. Pieces of the wall were torn away. Bits of the material used to build the concussion grenades were scattered about. In the aftermath of the latest assault, they were all motionless, listening for sounds which might indicate another attack. They could hear the wind moaning in the chimney, and the stirring of tree branches outside. But there were no more threatening noises – for now.

Ray lay supine in the back of the pickup truck. His face had begun to blister from the flintlock's powder burns. It was covered with grime and sweat. Dillart and Bobby tended to their buddy. Taking a bottle of whisky, Dillart tore off a piece of his T-shirt and soaked it in the booze. Then he carefully applied the alcohol-drenched rag to Ray's face. Ray winced in pain. Slowly, Dillart dabbed at

Ray's sensitive skin, wiping away the grime and disinfecting his wounds. Bobby found it hard to watch. This whole misadventure had become so futile to him. There was nothing to be gained as far as he was concerned. But no matter what he said, Ray and Dillart wouldn't listen. Ray was paying for it now. He didn't wish the burns on him; still, Ray had it coming.

'Let's get out of here,' Bobby urged Dillart and Ray, hoping that Ray would have learned something from his mistakes and listen to him this time. 'Let's just get out of here.'

Ray sat up in the truck. 'No!' he insisted as vehemently as ever. 'It's gone too far.'

Dillart wrung out the whisky rag and poured fresh alcohol onto the cloth. Ray braced himself for the sting. 'Whoever that guy inside is, he's better than we thought,' Dillart told them. 'But we still gotta take them out. Nothing's changed.'

Ray grabbed Dillart's hand, as if they were swearing a solemn pact. 'We gotta finish it.'

'Finish it!' Bobby explained, incredulous. 'How? They've got a gun now.'

Ray motioned Dillart to put the rag and the bottle of whisky aside. He was well enough to go back into action. 'Don't matter what they got,' he said, struggling to his feet. 'We got more.'

Bobby and Dillart exchanged mystified glances while Ray climbed out of the back of the truck and walked over to the cab. They could tell he was still in pain, but he was recovering faster than they thought he would. Ray turned and smiled back at them.

'I been saving it just in case it came to this,' Ray told them, reaching under the seat of the cab.

'Saving what?' Bobby asked. He and Dillart moved in to get a closer look.

Ray pulled out three sticks of dynamite.

'Where'd you get those?' asked Bobby.

'Construction job I did. They never missed 'em.'

Dillart grinned. 'Good work, Ray.'

Ray brandished the dynamite proudly. 'We wait for daybreak,' he told his comrades with the voice of authority, 'then we take them out.'

Huddled on the floor of the cabin, her body pressed against the wall, Melinda quaked with fear. The chill in the cold country air only aggravated her shaking. Although she hugged herself tightly to warm herself and calm her nerves, it had little effect. Her eyes roved around the ravaged interior of the cabin. Images of the gunfire flashed through her mind. She recalled Dillart forcing himself upon her earlier in the day. Then Jake's body. Would the nightmare end? Maybe. Maybe when they were dead.

'We're not gonna make it!' she screamed, breaking the silence and alarming McCall.

'Melinda!' McCall shouted at her, then stepped across the debris towards her shivering body.

Melinda dissolved into convulsive sobs. She buried her head in her arms. 'We're not,' she wailed loudly. 'We're going to end up just like Jake.'

Scott watched from beside the window. His father gently placed his hands on Melinda's shoulders. At first she jumped at his touch; moments later, she grew calmer. McCall's hands had a soothing effect. She felt safer. But not safe. Not yet. Then he held her tightly, and the hope that he could protect her was renewed, though her mind was still wracked with doubts and haunting terrors.

'That is *not* how we are going to end up,' the Equalizer assured her, speaking in a soft, assuring, fatherly tone. 'They will make one last desperate attempt, but we will survive it.'

'No,' said Melinda, bowing her head, doubtful she could face more violence or the horrible sounds of battle.

Scott continued to observe his father, as though he were studying the way he dealt with Melinda.

'Melinda, look at me,' McCall said. Tenderly, he lifted her chin. At last she and he were looking each other in the

161

eyes. 'You've been through a very difficult ordeal. You've been beaten down. But don't defeat yourself now. Let's not give them that advantage.' Melinda couldn't take her eyes from McCall. The confidence in them was riveting. 'Find the strength inside of you,' the Equalizer told her. 'It is there and it will get you through this.'

Melinda said nothing. She just stared, hypnotized by the power in McCall's clear eyes. She wanted so much to believe his words.

'Will you be okay?' McCall asked her after she failed to respond to him. Melinda nodded. She would weather this storm. She just wanted it to be over quickly.

McCall's advice to Melinda had a similar mesmerizing effect on his son Scott, who was captivated by both his father's sensitivity and his ability to draw on inner resources of strength. There was an important lesson about life to be learned from his dad's approach, Scott thought; in adversity, you sometimes have to dig deep for untested abilities. Already Scott was discovering things about himself that he'd never known, as well as recognizing traits he shared with his father. They were not so different as he imagined. Their separation had led him to believe that there was a gulf between them which could never be bridged. Through the time they'd shared, and through this bizarre emergency in the cabin, they'd both been forced into relying on each other in ways neither had foreseen.

Scott's mind was racing as fast as his adrenalin. His nerves were raw, making him sensitive to the slightest movements, sounds, feelings, and intonations in his father's voice. He noticed that Melinda remained jumpy. While McCall walked to peek out of a window, Scott stepped over towards Melinda. Wrapping his arms around her, he delicately raised her to her feet and walked her to the couch. Hoping for a moment's peace, they settled into the softness of the worn sofa. After sheltering themselves against the walls and the hard floor, it felt luxurious. Meanwhile, McCall continued to gaze towards the truck at the plotting threesome.

Scott decided the best approach to take with Melinda

would be to keep the conversation light; act as if nothing were out of the ordinary. They would all have a better chance if they could remove themselves somewhat from the tension of the situation.

'What do you want for dinner?' he asked Melinda. The question puzzled her. 'You like pizza?'

'What are you talking about?' she said, regarding him the way she would a lunatic.

'I'm talking about dinner,' Scott told her matter-of-factly. 'Aren't you hungry? Hasn't all this excitement worked up your appetite?'

Melinda caught on to Scott's new tack. She sighed, slumped deeper into the couch, and even managed a smile. 'I'm losing my mind,' she said. 'You know that don't you?' She laughed at the image of herself – trembling, crying, hysterical – and began to realize the humour in the situation.

'We're gonna make it,' Scott said with resolve, playfully punching her in the arm.

McCall turned and looked at the two of them on the couch. Scott was completing what he had started. Melinda was not only calmer. She was becoming relaxed. McCall saw in his son the ability to push beyond his own inhibitions, to transcend his emotions, and to stop concentrating on his needs and attend to the welfare of others. McCall was proud of him. He watched as the two kids, physically and emotionally exhausted, drifted off to sleep. They sat side by side, Scott's arm around Melinda.

The Equalizer was used to going without sleep. In stressful situations he'd stayed up for nights on end without losing any mental clarity or physical prowess. Tonight he would let Scott and Melinda sleep. They needed it; he didn't. He would stand guard at the window and alert them if anything happened. He doubted it would. Their attackers were tiring. Maybe they were regrouping, continuing the siege in a battle of wits.

All night long the Equalizer kept his vigil at the window. He expected the attack at dawn.

He was right.

TWENTY-SEVEN

Before it became strong enough to dissipate the grey morning mists, the sun rose behind the trees, casting pink streaks across the sky. Dew sparkled on the damp grass. Roosters crowed from a nearby farm. Somewhere in the distance a dog barked. But it was the birds with their constant early morning chirping that brought the dawn to life.

The black truck no longer sat ominously in front of the cabin. During the night, they had moved it farther back into the brush. Dillart, Ray and Bobby had taken turns sleeping and keeping watch. Unlike the occupants of the cabin, the three young men had no source of warmth. The autumn air was chilly. They had to huddle inside the cab to fend off the cold.

Scott and Melinda had slept fitfully during the night. Now that the morning light was coming through the cabin's windows, Scott rose from the couch where he'd been awake, thinking, for some time. McCall stood watch at the window, his eyes trying to detect any suspicious movement from the men in the truck.

Scott joined his father at the window. 'I'm trying to think from their point of view,' he told him.

McCall regarded Scott with admiration. 'That's the only way to win any game. You first have to understand what the other person is thinking and feeling.'

'Is that why you play chess with yourself?'

'We haven't had a chance to really talk about anything this weekend, have we? I know you have a lot of anger, and I understand how much of it is directed at me. You may even hate me.'

His father's serious tone and words took Scott aback. He wasn't expecting a heart-to-heart talk at this time of the morning, under these circumstances.

'Hate you? My God – I could never . . .' McCall seemed momentarily embarrassed at having raised the possibility that his son hated him. Scott became suddenly reflective. Looking deep into his father's eyes, he told him, 'When I was eight years old and you left – we were living across from the park. I'd go there and sit on this one special rock all by myself and try to figure out why my Daddy hates me. What did I do that was so bad it made him leave?'

'Oh, Scott,' said McCall, reaching out to touch his son's shoulder.

Scott shook his head. 'I didn't hate you for leaving. I guess it was me I hated. I figured there was something wrong with me because it had to be me. And those feelings that I had as an eight-year-old sitting on that rock are still very close to me.'

Tears welled up in McCall's eyes. Scott couldn't remember when he'd ever in his life seen his father cry.

'I always loved you, Scott.'

Scott, too, felt tears coming on. 'I know that now. I guess I've always known it. I just wish that love had had a higher priority. But I understand.'

Gazing at each other, their eyes locked with a powerful intensity, both of them struggling to keep from crying. Each wanted to embrace the other; each held back. Uncomfortable with the emotion surging through him, McCall finally turned and glanced at Melinda who remained

165

asleep on the couch. Scott turned also, looking out the of window to where the truck had been parked most of the night. Suddenly, he became excited and shouted to his father.

'Dad, they're gone!'

'I don't think so,' McCall told him. 'My guess is they'll make one last desperate move.' Suddenly business-like, McCall yelled to Melinda on the couch. 'Melinda!' Groggy she roused from her sleep. 'Get up. Cover the side window. We're not out of the woods yet.'

Disoriented, she rubbed the sleep from her eyes, took in the strange surroundings and, recalling the events of the past night, felt a twinge of apprehension setting in again.

The truck was nestled in a copse of trees whose thick foliage obscured it from view. The site was actually only a few yards away from the clearing where McCall's Jaguar sat, and where the truck itself had been the night before.

The night had taken its toll on the young marauders. All three were hung over from the enormous quantities of alcohol they'd consumed. Ray's burns weren't healed. They remained sensitive. He continued to drink to relieve the pain, and to fuel his blood lust. Ray had the last watch before sunrise; now that there was light outside, Ray roused his two sleeping comrades. They'd barely stirred from their sleep when Ray proposed his new game plan.

'I'm gonna ride the truck in!' Ray informed them. 'You two cover the rear.' Not quite awake, Dillart and Bobby exchanged confused glances as Ray elaborated. 'I'll meet you on the road when it's over.'

Following Ray's instructions, Dillart and Ray fanned out into the underbrush and moved towards the rear of the cabin. Ray took the sticks of dynamite and hopped into the cab. His vision of the cabin blowing sky high gave him an added burst of energy. This was just like the war movies Ray had seen in which one guy rides in and saves the company. Why, the way Ray felt, he could whip a whole platoon of Viet Cong single-handedly. Move over, Rambo . . . he started up the truck.

*   *   *

Inside the cabin, McCall was poised by the window. The automatic rifle was in his hands, ready for action should the three launch a surprise attack. Scott peered out of the window. His eye glimpsed movement outside.

'One of them is over here,' Scott said, motioning to his father.

The figure Scott had spied was Bobby, who moved through the underbrush in the woods behind the house. Scott could even make out the noise of the crisp autumn leaves rustling under his feet. Bobby could stand to learn a few scouting tricks from the Indians, Scott thought. McCall wasn't surprised. Bobby was a rank amateur.

'This is just what I figured would happen,' McCall told Scott.

Staring more intently into the depths of the underbrush beyond the clearing, the Equalizer saw the glint of the sun striking the truck's windshield. If the sun hadn't given the pickup away, the sound of its engine revving would have. Suddenly the truck exploded to life. Its big back tyres gripped the dirt and pushed the truck forward, spitting earth and making short work of the reeds and brush in its path.

Alerted to the imminent danger, McCall shouted to Scott and Melinda. 'Get ready.' He motioned to his son, yelling, 'Scott, the trap door.' Scott scurried to the trap door which led to the crawl space and yanked it up. 'Both of you,' McCall continued, keeping an eye on the oncoming truck. 'Get down there, and stay under the cabin.'

Holding the door, Scott helped Melinda as she scooted into the crawl space. 'Now,' McCall screamed at Scott. 'Get out now.' Scott followed Melinda into the crawl space. Once under the floor of the cabin, he shoved her down against the cold earth. Their bodies lying against the ground, they could sense the truck's vibrations as it sped towards the cabin.

As the truck came at the house and into McCall's range, he opened fire. The gun spit out a barrage of bullets, hitting the truck and cutting into the ground around it. The

Equalizer could tell that one bullet had struck the radiator. It erupted in a cloud of steam. But the truck kept coming, veering towards the cabin, as if the driver had lost control. Then McCall saw Ray lighting something – a dynamite fuse. Seconds later, Ray let loose with the dynamite, hurling it out of the window. The stick soared towards the cabin's front porch. On seeing the dynamite hit the porch, McCall dashed to the trap door.

The truck spun around, kicking up a cloud of dirt alongside the cabin. Ray floored it to get away before the blast tore the cabin apart. He gunned the accelerator. Steam poured from the front hood. He clenched his teeth in anger and frustration and began to swear. But he was lucky. Though sputtering from its wounds, the truck made it before the cabin blew.

Ray saw the blast in his rear-view mirror. He could feel the concussion of air against the back of his neck as he pulled the truck away. The explosion shook everything in the area, including the trees. Patches of screaming, frightened birds clouded the sky as they beat their wings wildly and flew off.

The cabin went up like a tinderbox. Logs sailed through the air in all directions. After the dynamite ripped the walls and roof apart, the fire began to consume the structure in a gigantic ball of flame. Underneath the cabin, Scott, Melinda, and McCall huddled together. They couldn't help hearing the deafening roar of the dynamite or feeling the impact of the blast. But they had been spared its lethal power. Melinda screamed, but her cry was more than drowned out by the noise of the explosion.

Not far behind them, Bobby was knocked to the ground by the power of the blast. He had a sinking feeling in the pit of his stomach. He was a murderer now. He would have to live with the guilt of this for the rest of his life; that is, if someone didn't catch him and put him behind bars forever. There wasn't much time for thinking right now. Bobby had to scramble to his feet, find Dillart, and get the hell out of there. He spotted Dillart across the remains of the house which was now engulfed in flames.

'It's over,' Bobby shouted over the crackling noise. 'Let's get out of here.'

Dillart ran around and joined Bobby, and the two beat a path through the woods towards the road where they desperately hoped Ray would still be waiting. But when they got there, they couldn't find him, at least not immediately.

'Where'd he go?' asked Dillart, scared and impatient.

Then they heard a hissing sound further off in the wooded area.

'There!' Bobby said, pointing towards the truck. Even through the heavy brush, he could see the steam pouring from its radiator. It was a sickening sound.

Out of breath and sweaty, Bobby and Dillart reached Ray, who stood by the truck. He looked spent and disheartened. They didn't have to ask him if the truck was dead. They read the bad news in his face.

They could afford only a moment to rest. Someone was bound to notice the explosion and the fire any moment, and they couldn't risk being seen in the vicinity. Once the police discovered the bodies, there would be patrol men and dogs combing the area for suspects and evidence.

Suddenly the odds didn't seem to be on their side anymore. Their luck had died with the truck. Making a clean getaway on foot wasn't going to be easy. But they had to give it a shot. They had no other choice.

Dillart led the way through the woods. Already weary from too much drink and too little sleep, they staggered through the brush. Branches scraped their faces and blocked their path. Progress was slow. Every so often, they glanced back at the plume of black smoke rising above the trees. Someone was bound to have seen it by now. Imagining the breath of the law down their necks, they pushed onward.

Sheriff Sam Stone began the day routinely enough with his customary drive to work along the main highway of King's Harbor. He was about to make the turn and drive straight into town when his eye caught the black smoke spiralling upward above the trees. At the sight of the smoke, he brought his car to a sudden halt and reached for his radio.

'Break, break, bellyacher,' he shouted into the phone. The alarm would bring help right away. In the meantime, the sheriff decided to head towards the source of the smoke. Somebody might need his help.

Not far from the road, sandwiched between the highway and the cabin, was a slope which led down to the road. Dillart was sure they could get away safely if they could only make the road. His two comrades took Dillart at his word, though there wasn't much logic in his thinking. Reaching the road would only place them out in the open and make them more vulnerable. Besides, the cops would be able to trace the owner of the truck from its licence plate. The threesome had left in such a hurry that they didn't think about destroying the truck or the plates. Their minds had surrendered to fear and impulse.

They crashed through the last thicket of brush before the road and let out a victorious whoop. The highway lay before them. There wasn't a car on it. The slope leading down to the pavement was steep and covered with pine needles, leaves, and twigs. They tried walking sideways down the hill, but all three eventually gave up on walking, and slid or tumbled down.

Upon reaching the road, they got to their feet and brushed themselves off. They were so elated to have come this far that they failed to notice the car coming around the bend. Its red light was flashing. Sheriff Stone had them all in view.

Dillart wasn't thinking clearly; for that matter, neither were Bobby and Ray. They had no reason to assume that the sheriff was after them in connection with the fire. But their guilt made them jump to that conclusion. Seeing his car approach, they immediately turned and ran up the slope, digging their heels into the damp earth as they climbed back the way they had come.

They hadn't gotten very far when they saw the figure of

170

the Equalizer atop the ridge. Like a sentinel, he stood there with his rifle pointed directly at the three of them. If they had any hope of escape, their hopes were dashed as they swung around and saw the sheriff's car pulling up onto the shoulder of the highway. Doom was written on their faces. The fight went out of them. They sunk to the ground in surrender.

Atop the hill, Scott walked Melinda towards his father. The dramatic twenty-four hours had not only drawn him and his father together; he felt a special closeness to Melinda as well. Although he knew it couldn't endure – that it was just a strong emotional bonding brought about by life-threatening, bizarre circumstances – he was reluctant to let go of her so soon. He wished there were time to get to know her before he went off to Paris. But he knew the wish was unrealistic.

His arms around Melinda, Scott gave her support as she looked down the slope at her three tormentors. Justice had been done, thanks to Scott and McCall. She had a great sense of satisfaction – and gratitude towards the father and son who had saved her life.

'It's over,' Scott told her softly, taking her in his arms and embracing her. Melinda smiled, and sagged in relief against him.

McCall gave Melinda the fare to Toronto. She and Scott promised to write. He doubted she would; then again, she might. Scott was eager to leave Maine and return to New York. He and his father drove out of town in the Jaguar as soon as Sheriff Stone had taken their statements and Melinda's. Their testimony would be enough to put their three tormentors away for several years.

Scott didn't remember much about the drive back to the city. He slept most of the way. The rest of the time, both he and his father were quiet, reflective. He knew his father wouldn't want to talk much about their weekend ordeal. It wasn't his nature. Already the Equalizer had assigned the experience to a file in the past. Scott didn't hold that against him. Living for the present had certain advantages. You didn't hurt as much from the past, for one thing; on the other hand, you ran the risk of losing touch with your emotions. Scott tried to imagine his father's profession as being something like his own dedication to music. When Scott concentrated on playing the violin, there was no other world besides the music and the emotions it summoned up inside him. His father needed a different set of skills, many of them involving survival and violence. Scott tried to see how his father's commitment to people was no less important than his own commitment to music. For the moment, he could refrain from judging his father's occupation in a negative light. For the moment, Scott felt love. He could afford to be generous in his judgements.

The next two days sped by. Scott's mother Janice wined and dined her son, squeezing every last ounce of time from his busy schedule. Though she did her best to be cheerful and charming, her separation anxiety was evident. Scott tried to laugh about it, but he was feeling the same way himself. He was still apprehensive about being on his own. But having experienced a literal trial by fire with his father, he realized it was silly to be apprehensive about the Strasbourg Conservatory. After all, they wouldn't throw dynamite at him if they didn't like his violin playing.

McCall picked Scott up at his mother's apartment, carried his bags down to the Jag, and drove him on the expressway to Kennedy Airport. They said little to each other along the way. Scott turned around and looked out of the back window at the receding skyline of Manhattan as if he were committing it to memory. A thrill went through him as he was buoyed by the sudden awareness that he was taking the first big step in pursuing his dreams. He wondered if his father had ever felt this way; if there was ever anything he had cared about this passionately. Maybe his dad's dream and his were beginning simultaneously. There wasn't time to find out now.

The traffic was unusually light at the airport. McCall had no trouble finding a parking space in the lot by the inter-

172

national building. He and Scott shared the burden of carrying the baggage into the terminal. Both stared straight ahead.

By the time Scott had checked his bags and received his seat allocation, his flight was being called for boarding. McCall walked him to the security desk.

'Better go,' McCall told his son when they announced boarding of this flight a second time.

Scott seemed reluctant. 'Yeah,' he smiled tightly. 'I'll be home for the holidays. Will you keep the back room?'

'It will be ready for you.'

Scott and his father regarded each other for a long moment, then Scott set his carry-on luggage on the ground and gave McCall a big hug. His eyes began to cloud with tears.

'I'm gonna miss you, Dad.'

'I'm gonna miss you, son.'

Scott thought again about the moments of emotional intimacy he'd wanted to share with his father and hadn't.

'I wish that . . .' Scott began, his voice catching.

'I know,' said his father. 'So do I.'

Each turned to go his own way, not noticing that the other was openly wiping away the tears.

STAR BOOKS BESTSELLERS

FICTION

SHATTER	John Farris	£1.50*
REVENGE OF MORIARTY	John Gardner	£2.25
GOLGOTHA	John Gardner	£1.95
BACK OF THE TIGER	Jack Gerson	£1.95
SPECTRE OF MARALINGA	Michael Hughes	£1.95
DEBT OF HONOUR	Adam Kennedy	£1.95
DEATH MAIL	Peter Leslie	£1.95
CONDOR	Thomas Luke	£2.50*
AIRSHIP	Peter MaCalan	£2.50
IKON	Graham Masterton	£2.50*
HAWL	James Peacock	£1.95
DOG SOLDIERS	Robert Stone	£1.95

STAR Books are obtainable from many booksellers and newsagents. If you have any difficulty tick the titles you want and fill in the form below.

Name _____

Address _____

_____

Send to: Star Books Cash Sales, P.O. Box 11, Falmouth, Cornwall, TR10 9EN.

Please send a cheque or postal order to the value of the cover price plus: UK: 55p for the first book, 22p for the second book and 14p for each additional book ordered to the maximum charge of £1.75.

BFPO and EIRE: 55p for the first book, 22p for the second book, 14p per copy for the next 7 books, thereafter 8p per book.

OVERSEAS: £1.00 for the first book and 25p per copy for each additional book.

While every effort is made to keep prices low, it is sometimes necessary to increase prices at short notice. Star Books reserve the right to show new retail prices on covers which may differ from those advertised in the text or elsewhere.

*NOT FOR SALE IN CANADA

STAR BOOKS BESTSELLERS

CHILLERS

COME THE NIGHT	Nick Blake	£1.95
SHADOWS	Shaun Hutson	£2.25
SLUGS	Shaun Hutson	£1.95
SPAWN	Shaun Hutson	£1.80
EREBUS	Shaun Hutson	£2.25
SLIMER	Harry Adam Knight	£1.80
THE PARIAH	Graham Masterton	£2.25*
THE PLAGUE	Graham Masterton	£1.80*
THE SPHINX	Graham Masterton	£1.50*
THE DJINN	Graham Masterton	£1.50*
THE MANITOU	Graham Masterton	£1.50*
THE DONORS	Horvitz & Gerhard	£1.95*
THE SENTINEL	Jeffrey Konvitz	£1.65*
HALLOWEEN III	Jack Martin	£1.80*

STAR Books are obtainable from many booksellers and newsagents. If you have any difficulty tick the titles you want and fill in the form below.

Name _____

Address _____

_____

Send to: Star Books Cash Sales, P.O. Box 11, Falmouth, Cornwall, TR10 9EN.

Please send a cheque or postal order to the value of the cover price plus:
UK: 55p for the first book, 22p for the second book and 14p for each additional book ordered to the maximum charge of £1.75.

BFPO and EIRE: 55p for the first book, 22p for the second book, 14p per copy for the next 7 books, thereafter 8p per book.

OVERSEAS: £1.00 for the first book and 25p per copy for each additional book.

While every effort is made to keep prices low, it is sometimes necessary to increase prices at short notice. Star Books reserve the right to show new retail prices on covers which may differ from those advertised in the text or elsewhere.

*NOT FOR SALE IN CANADA